Susan Gates

SCHOLASTIC
PRESS

Scholastic Children's Books,
Commonwealth House, 1–19 New Oxford Street
London WC1A 1NU, UK
a division of Scholastic Ltd
London ~ New York ~ Toronto ~ Sydney ~ Auckland

First published by Scholastic Ltd, 1997

ISBN 0 590 54293 1

Typeset by DP Photosetting, Aylesbury, Bucks
Printed by Cox & Wyman Ltd, Reading Berks

10 9 8 7 6 5 4 3 2 1

Chapter One
Maths

PASS TO KATY B. PRIVATE!

Katy B, this is the 2nd note I've sent you! Stop doing your maths, you swot, this is much more important. Don't worry, Spenser's not looking. He's explaining something to Sophie. Trust her. Look at her nodding and grinning. She's always greasing round teachers, isn't she?

Anyway, will you do it, Katy? What I wrote in my last note? Please, please, please! Will you ask Cooper (drool, drool!) if he'll go out with me.

Lisa, you pest, I'm trying to work out what angle c is in this triangle. Your love life isn't the most important thing in the world, you know! Stop writing me notes. I'll talk to you at break. Signed Katy B.

Katy, don't be a swot and a spoilsport. I can't wait until break. I've got to know NOW. Just look at him at the back next to Ant. He's got his chair tipped back and his boots on his desk. Isn't he truly gorgeous? Please Katy B, write Cooper a note NOW. I can't send it, can I? That's what best friends are for. I'll even write it for you. Just cut along the dotted lines.

✂- -

Cooper, do you want to go out with Lisa?

	TICK HERE
YES	
NO	
I'LL THINK ABOUT IT.	

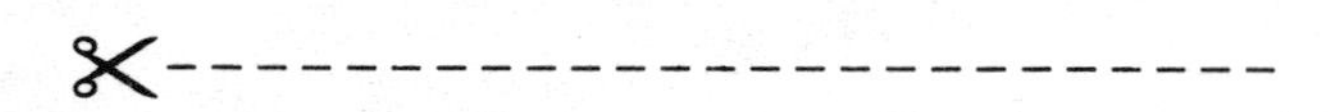

What is angle c anyway? I can't work it out.

37 degrees. Lisa, I told you, I'm busy. No more notes! But you're right though, he is gorgeous. All the girls fancy him. But I thought he was still meeting Emily? Watch out, girl! Emily's 100% rock hard. She's scary.

She lifts weights. If you tried to take him off her, you'd be dead. Signed *Katy B.*

It's OK Katy, he dumped her. Yes he did! Ant told me. Ant says he was glad to get rid of her. So, quick Katy B, before someone else grabs him. Mmmmm, just look at that blond hair, those muscles. Is he a hunk or what? Some people say he's crazy. But I don't care, I like crazy people! At least they're not boring. Not like Rachel and Dexter. Yawn, yawn, aren't they boring? They've been going out for THREE WHOLE YEARS. Ever since Year 7! That's not just boring. That is truly sick. Anyway, what's wrong with Rachel today? Her eyes are all red. Has she been crying? PS. Someone said you met Jonathan Prescott last night. Tell me it's not true! You can do better than him, Katy. Let me find someone for you. He wears clothes from Oxfam and his mum is a school cleaner and he keeps rabbits! Black and white ones with pink goggly eyes. It's embarrassing!

Lisa, you are a bitch sometimes, even if you are my best friend. His mum is a really nice lady – I've met her. So what if they don't have much money? They can't help— can't write any more. Old Spenser's nosing around. Signed *Katy B.*

FOR COOPER. STRICTLY PRIVATE

You'll be surprised when you open this note, Cooper. It's from Katy B. I'm sending it for Lisa. She really likes you. She wants to know if you'll go out with her. So will you? Please tick and pass back.

YES	
NO	
I'LL THINK ABOUT IT	
I'M STILL MEETING EMILY	

PASS TO KATY B. ANYONE TOUCHES THIS NOTE THEY'RE DEAD

YES	✓
NO	
I'LL THINK ABOUT IT	
I'M STILL MEETING EMILY	That bitch you must be joking

Katy B, this note is from Rachel. Can U see the splodges on my note:

Count them up. There R seven of them. They R my tears. I need some advice. About me and Dexter. I need some advice RIGHT NOW. I'm so confused!

Hi, Katy B! Guess who this note is from? Yes, it's from ME, Sophie ☺ I know you are clever, Katy B. You are the cleverest person in the world, the galaxy, the universe. So can you tell me the answer to question 2, part b? How long is the perimeter? I asked Spenser. Did you see me? But I didn't understand a word he said even though I said I did. He is useless. And he's got hairs coming out of his nose. So tell me the answer Katy B. From Sophie ☺ your bestest friend.

You passed Cooper a note just now. I saw you! And he passed it back. What did he tick, Katy B? Did he tick yes? Did he? Did he? Did he?
PS. Course, I don't care if he didn't.

PASS THIS NOTE TO

1. **Lisa**
2. **Sophie**
3. **Rachel**

I'm getting really mad now! Will you 3 stop sending me notes. I've got to finish my maths. I'll talk to you all at break. DON'T SEND ANY MORE NOTES.

Signed Katy B.

Chapter Two
Geography

PASS TO KATY B. PRIVATE!

Want to know what happened when I went out with Cooper last night? Bet you do. Bet you're dying to know! What's an isthmus look like?

Not NOW Lisa. Too risky writing notes in Geog. We'll get detention. Wait until English.
It looks like this:

isthmus

Signed Katy B.

Chapter Three

English

FOR KATY B

It's OK Katy, I can write loads now. Mrs Potts will think I'm doing my Romeo and Juliet essay.

Well, last night was brilliant. A funny thing happened before I went out with Cooper though. I was putting my make-up on and the phone rang and it was for me of course and it was Ant. I didn't even think he knew where I lived. Anyway, guess what he said? He said, "Lisa, I've always really fancied you. How about going out with me and ditching Cooper?" I nearly dropped the phone! I was flattered because Ant is quite good-looking, isn't he? But I was really surprised because Ant is supposed to be Cooper's best mate. So I was thinking what to say when I heard someone laugh down the phone. I said, "Is anyone with you, Ant? Is Cooper with you?" And Ant said, "No, there's no one here." But I'm sure I heard Cooper laughing. So I said, "No Ant, I can't go out with you. I can't two-time Cooper." And then Ant said something really strange. He said, "Lucky for you, that's the right answer."

What do you think about that, Katy B? Do you think Cooper and Ant were playing a game or something? Whoops! Pottsie's checking up on us. And I haven't even written the essay title! Write me an answer quick.

Sounds like a funny kind of game to me, Lisa. Sounds like some stupid test. Like Cooper got Ant to phone, to see if you'd two-time him or not. Don't like it. It's sneaky. Signed Katy B.

Phew, Pottsie's gone. I'm sick of her – she keeps interrupting my note writing. Katy B, you do take things serious. You worry too much! Coop and Ant were just messing about. Anyway, that's not important. Guess what Cooper did last night? He's mad, honestly! We were just hanging around, you know, outside Pizza Hut and Ant turned up and Cooper said, "Watch this." And he put three matches between his fingers and Ant lit them for him. And I said, "Don't, you'll burn yourself!" But do you know what he did, Katy? He just watched the matches burn right down and his face was like stone and I said, "Stop it, stop it!" But he said, "This is a test. So I don't feel pain. I don't feel anything." But he must have done because his skin was all blisters. He's really brave isn't he? And after that he was really nice to me cos he could see I was upset. He said, "Cheer up. I only did it for a laugh!"

But that's really weird, Lisa. Honestly, don't YOU think that's weird? Are you sure you want to see him again? That thing he did with the matches makes me shiver. Signed Katy B.

Katy, don't try and spoil things! Not now I've got a drop-dead gorgeous boyfriend! You're jealous aren't you? Just cos I'm going out with COOPER and you've only got that boring little creep J Prescott (yawn, yawn) who keeps rabbits.

PASS TO J PRESCOTT. CONFIDENTIAL!
J, this is from Katy B. What do you think about Cooper? Lisa's just started going out with him.

I think he's bad news. I think he's trouble. He scares me to death. He'd scare anyone to death who'd got any sense. He's got cold eyes.

Anyway, I thought Emily was still going out with him?

Want to come round my house tonight Katy? My mum will be there. She says come for your tea. If you want to, that is. J.

I just wrote a note to Jonathan. About you going out with Cooper. And he thinks Cooper is trouble. He thinks he's bad news. Honest, Lisa, I know Cooper's gorgeous and everything but do you really want to go out with him again? Signed Katy B.

Katy! I am so mad I could scream! Who cares what Prescott thinks? Prescott is a pathetic person. How dare you tell my PERSONAL AND PRIVATE business to someone like that? I thought you were my best friend? I'm not going to write you any more notes. I'm not going to speak to you at break. I'm so mad my hands are shaking – look my writing's gone all wobbly.

PASS TO THAT PATHETIC PERSON J PRESCOTT

Prescott, this is from Lisa Hutchinson. How dare you say Cooper is bad news? He is a zillion times better than you. You are not in the same league! Who do you think you are, saying things about him? If you don't watch out I will tell him and then you will be dead! And, anyway, you don't think Katy B is going out with you because she LIKES you, do you? I mean, have you looked in a mirror lately? I know she is my friend and she is supposed to be brainy but she is too soft-hearted. She feels sorry for people. And she is only going out with you because she feels SORRY for you. Why else would she be doing it?

Hi, Katy B, guess who? Yes, it's me, Sophie ☺. I can see all these notes criss-crossing all over the place. You have passed them to Lisa and Jonathan. What about ME? I want to get a note too. Go on, please, please, please, send ME a note before Pottsie stops doing her marking.

J, I'd like to come round to your house tonight. Is 6 o'clock OK? Write me a note, quick, say yes or no. Signed Katy B.

Katy, where were U yesterday? This note is from Rachel! Remember me, >Rachel<? U promised you'd talk to me at break about my problems. U know, with Dexter. But I looked for U everywhere and you just disappeared. U were not anywhere! It was as if U were hiding from me!

Anyway, I have got U now so here's my problem.

U know Dexie and me have been going out, like FOREVER?

U know we see each other every single night?

U know I have got his ring and he's got mine?

Well, he's been really strange lately, picking fights with me all the time. He even said, "I've got to mend my bike Friday." And he knows we babysit for my auntie on Friday. We always do. We've been doing it, like FOREVER.

So what is going on Katy B? Write me a note quick, give me some advice. U are smart. U always know what to do.

PS. I can't think of a single thing to write about Romeo and Juliet. I am useless at English.

Rach, how can I do this essay with all these notes whizzing around? I don't know, why don't you and Dexie hang around with some other people? I don't mean two-time each other or anything. But why don't you go out with your mates? And Dexie go out with his mates? Just SOMETIMES. I mean, don't you run out of things to talk about? I mean, it's always RachelandDexie, like you're one person. That's a bit claustrophobic, isn't it?

Anyway, can you do me a favour? I'm putting a note in with your note. It's for Jonathan. Look, he is sitting right near you. Can you make sure he gets it? I sent him a note just now but I don't think he got it as he

didn't pass me one back. So just pass him this one, will you. Thanks. *Katy B.*

J, is 6 o'clock OK for tonight? And cheer up! You look really miserable! Signed *Katy B.*

Don't use big words, Katy please. I am not brainy like U R. What does claustrothingy mean anyway? I just passed Jonathan your note like U asked me to. He tore it up in teeny little pieces and threw it away. Why did he do that?

Hi, Katy B! Yes, it's me again, your pal Sophie. ☺ I will get very cross in a minute. You haven't sent me a single note yet. Everyone is getting them but me. People will think that I'm not popular! Look, I've made it easy for you. I've written you a note to send to me. So all you have to do is tear it off and send it back. See, easy peasy. Here it is:

Hi, Sophie. Have a nice day!

Jonathan, what's the matter? Don't tear this note up please. Why are you staring at me like you hate me? Just tell me what's going on! *Katy B.*

Chapter 4
Art

I was mad at first at what U said about me and Dexie being, what was that long word you used? But then I thought, well, Katy B is supposed to be a wise person and me and Dexie are fighting all the time so I will try out what she says. It can't make things worse. But I am writing this note to tell U it was a total disaster!

Pass me a dark green when U send me a note back will U? I am useless at Art and why do we have to draw plants? Plants are dead boring, why can't we have a male model or something?

Anyway, I did what you said about seeing different people and at the weekend when I saw Dexie I invited Sophie along too. Well, Dexie was mad and he said, "What did you invite HER for?" and I said, "She says she's my best friend." And he started insulting her and saying she's a bubblebrain and will spoil things – so naturally I had to stick up for her because she's my best friend, isn't she? But then, after we'd said all this, we were walking through the cemetery where we usually go. There is a gravestone there that makes me cry, have U seen it? It is for the boy who got killed on his motorbike last year and it has always got fresh flowers on it and it says IN MEMORY OF PETER, EIGHTEEN YEARS, OUR DEAR, DEAR SON, SO TRAGICALLY TAKEN FROM US ALWAYS IN OUR HEARTS. So I was crying over it like I always do when I saw Dexie round the back of Peter's gravestone giving Sophie a kiss. After what he said about her being a bubblebrain and me saying she isn't she gets Grade As all the time! I'm yelling, "What R U 2 doing?" and Dexie says, "It's not what it looks like, I just stumbled and hit her lips with mine." So I say, "Oh yeah. Oh YEAH! I was not born yesterday U know. I am not a COMPLETE idiot! Do U expect me to believe that?" Then Dexie says, "Believe what U like." And I say, "Do U want us to finish?" and he shrugs and says, "All right then." So I say, "All right then!" So he says, "All right!" Then he storms off. And I storm off but before I do I throw his ring in a litter bin and I have to search for it afterwards in a big mess of curry sauce and chips and half-eaten cheeseburgers. It was gross. So now Dexie and me have broken up after we've been going out, like FOREVER and I'm not talking to Sophie either on account of her kissing him behind Peter's gravestone. She said she was my best friend. How could she do that? So I've got no boyfriend and no best friend. My life is a mess, it is tragic. So what am I going to do Katy B?

PS. Pass me a red as well so I can colour in the plant pot.

PPS. I should have known all this was going to happen. On Saturday my horoscope said: "U must beware of friends betraying you." How true!

PPPS. I was thinking about getting DEXIE tattooed on my ankle in a little heart. Like this:

It's cute, isn't it? There is a place down an alley near the shopping mall that does it. But I'm certainly NOT going to have it done now.

PPPPS. I bet I start smoking again cos I am so worked up and it will calm me down and it's all your fault that I am so depressed and now I have spent half the lesson writing this stupid note and I have not finished my plant and I will get killed by Miss Forsythe when she comes round to check our work.

This is me. I am really miserable, it is the worst day of my life.

So write me an answer quick!

Just because your life is in a mess, Rach, you can't depend on me to sort it out. When I said, "Go round with some other people," I didn't mean make a threesome with Sophie on a date. That's asking for trouble! And anyway, why does everyone ask me to sort out their problems? I am not an agony auntie you know! I've got enough problems of my own thank you and no one helps me with mine! Actually you may like to know that I'm in exactly the same situation as you. My best

friend Lisa is not speaking to me and J is ignoring me as well and tearing up my notes but don't ask me why. And don't you dare use me as an excuse to start smoking again. It's your own stupid fault if you do that. Your choice – nothing to do with me. Signed Katy B.

Katy B, U sound really mad! I have never known U like that, U are usually Miss Super Cool. Never mind, I will sort out your life 4 U. Just leave it to good ol' Rach. I will be ever so tactful, honest. PS. If Dexie does not make up I will try to make him jealous by going out with that boy in Year 11. I don't know his name but he has a nose like this and hair like this. Do U know who I mean? If U do, will U ask him 4 me?

PASS TO RACHEL. URGENT!!

Rach, thanks for the offer but no thanks. Don't try to help me. Please! Don't interfere. OK? PROMISE me you won't – I can sort out my own problems, really I can. By the way, I don't think making Dexie jealous is a very good idea.

FOR J PRESCOTT. URGENT!!!!

Prescott this note is from Rachel. What are U playing at you sick person? Why are U ignoring Katy B? She is a dead nice girl and does not deserve to be treated like that. Tell me immediately or I will tell Cooper what Lisa says U said about him and he will break both your legs. U will be dogmeat!

See, Katy B, U are not the only brain box who can sort things out. I have just written a really tactful note to J Prescott and he has just replied that Lisa told him that U were only seeing him because U felt sorry for him. I wrote a note back and told him not to be so stupid, that Lisa is a well-known bitch and he had better make it up with U really quick. So expect a note from him any second now.
PS. My plant looks a mess – it is a green splodge. I will tell Miss Forsythe that is how I see it. Then she will think I am dead artistic!

Sorry, Katy, I shouldn't have taken notice of what Lisa wrote. Please will you still come round my house tonight? Six o'clock is OK. My mum likes you a lot. Except, I don't get it, why do you have Lisa as a friend when she goes and writes things like that behind your back and tries to break us up? J.

No you shouldn't have taken notice of what Lisa wrote! But I will come round tonight. 6 o'clock.

Can't explain about Lisa. Don't know why I put up with her myself sometimes. She's spoiled and selfish

but other times she's really kind and funny. She's been my best friend since nursery school, since toddler group even. She drives me crazy a lot of the time but I still like her. And anyway, she needs looking after. She's pretty and popular and used to everyone loving her and doing what she wants. But she can't take care of herself so I have to take care of her or she'll get hurt. She's like a little girl really. Besides, she isn't all bad. She's really generous sometimes. She would lend me her clothes any time I liked only her clothes do not fit me as she's got a much better figure. See you tonight then. Signed Katy B.

Dexie, this is from Katy B. I owe Rach a big favour so I'm writing you this note. She says everything is messed up between you and her and it's probably my fault because of a note I wrote her. It'd take too long to explain and Miss Forsythe is breathing down my neck. But just make it up with Rachel please. Write back on this piece of paper what you have decided. Just YES or NO or MAYBE will do. Katy B.

YES, NO, MAYBE. I dunno. Just tell Rach I'm thinking about it. And I did not kiss Sophie honest. She kissed me before I could stop her. She has tried to do it before – she chased me round the computer suite once. She is a really fast runner.

Katy! I have decided to write to you again even though you don't deserve it cos you told my private affairs, about me and Cooper, to that creep Prescott.

What a cheek! Old furface Forsythe just said my plant was rubbish. Did you hear her? I spent ages on that. She says I am SCATTERBRAINED and CARELESS. She gave me a D! Well I say she is an old witch. Someone told me they caught her kissing Mr Spenser in the Maths stock cupboard. But I don't believe it, do you? Just take a sneaky look at her top lip. Go on, do it now. See, she's got a little moustache, like Hitler. Fancy kissing that. YEUCH! Someone should tell her about hair removing cream.

She can see me writing but I don't care. I want to tell you about me and Coop. I was going to the Roller Disco with him on Saturday but now he says he cannot go because of having to go somewhere else. I was mad at first but then he got angry and said: "Make sure you behave yourself when I'm not there. Don't dance with any boys. Don't even speak to any boys. If you do, I'll know about it." Isn't that sweet? He's soooo jealous he must really like me. I know he is joking of course as how can I go to a disco and not dance with anyone? It'll ruin my reputation. Everyone will think I'm not popular any more! Anyway, if Cooper says anything, I can manage him. I can twist him round my little finger, just you see.

He scared me though on Saturday when he did something like the matches, only worse. He said, "I bet you don't believe that I'll cut my arm with this knife." So I just start laughing. I say, "Don't be stupid." So then he gets angry and says: "What, are you saying you don't believe me?" And, honest, Katy, he cut himself, right there in the middle of the street. Slashed his arm. It starts bleeding like mad, splashing down on to the pavement in big drops and I'm screaming but Ant, who was with us, just laughs and says, "Cooper, you're a real psycho. You should be locked up."

Still, I like crazy people, don't you Katy? At least they are not boring. You never know what they are going to do next, do you?

So, what shall I wear to the Roller Disco? I've got nothing to wear! I can't wear that new blue dress again cos I wore it last week and everyone has already seen me in it.

What do you mean you have got nothing to wear? You've got wardrobes full of stuff. Did he really cut himself Lisa? That's scary, I don't like that. Don't you think it's scary? Keep away from him. Promise me you will. Signed Katy B.

Honestly Katy, you take things serious. You worry too much. He was probably just showing off. Just acting tough. It was only a little cut. Anyway, what can I wear? I know! I will get my dad to give me some more money. You can come with me to the shopping mall Friday after school to help me choose something new.

Ant, this is Coop. I want to know who Lisa talks to, who she dances with at the Roller Disco. Right? Every move she makes I want to know about it. Right? Let's see if she can pass this test so easy.

Eat this note after you've read it. Let me see you eat it.

Chapter Five
Science

Help, Katy B. I can't do this stupid science test. What are the products of fractional distillation of crude oil? Are we supposed to have done that? I can't remember doing that! Pass me the answers quickly. Don't let Mr Walker see you. I'm seeing Coop tonight and do not want a detention. Went to the Roller Disco last night.

Petroleum gases, gasoline, naphtha, kerosene, gas oil, lubricating oil, bitumen. Lisa you pest! Don't write me any more notes until the end of the test.
Signed Katy B.

Thanks thanks thanks Katy, you saved my life in that test. Again! You are a swot though, aren't you? You always know the right answers. Anyway, Sophie says she will set up the experiment for me while I write you this teeny weeny note. She greases round everyone, doesn't she? The

Roller Disco was really brilliant. Everybody who was anybody was there. Except for Cooper of course. But Ant was there and all the other friends Coop hangs around with. I danced every single dance. And I wore those new black shiny trousers. You know the ones I nagged my dad for that cost a fortune that we got at the shopping mall. Except I don't know why it's called a Roller Disco cos nobody wears Roller boots. I danced with Ant and talked to loads of other boys. Actually it was better Cooper wasn't there as I could dance with anyone I liked. I get fed up dancing with just one person, don't you? And anyway, Cooper hates dancing. Why weren't you there? I know, don't tell me. You were revising for the science test, you swot!

I wasn't actually, I was round at J's and me and his mum were talking for ages about all sorts of things. I like her. It's funny but I can tell her things I wouldn't tell my own mum. Signed Katy B.

I don't tell my mum anything. She'd have a fit if she found out what I got up to. She still thinks I'm a sweet innocent little girl! Ha, ha, if only she knew. But seriously, Katy B. I mean seriously, you can't be getting serious with Prescott. By the way, did he show you his bunnies yet?

I'm not going to write you any more about me and J, Lisa, you'll only make jokes about it. Besides, he does not have black and white rabbits with pink eyes like you said. Those are Himalayan rabbits. J's got one rabbit. She's a Belgian hare. They're called that cos they look like hares, they've got long brown bodies and really long ears. She's beautiful. She's not tame at all or cuddly but very nervous and twitchy, like a wild hare is. J's made a run for her, he lets her out. You ought to see her jump and race about! She's having babies soon and J said I could have one if I liked.

Oh God, Katy B, yawn, yawn. Don't tell me you're a rabbit expert now. It is too pathetic. You will soon be a fully paid up member of the pathetic person's club if you don't watch out and then I won't be able to be best friends with you any more as it will ruin my reputation.

Chapter Six

Maths

FOR LISA URGENT!

Lisa, where were you before lessons? I wanted to talk to you. Sophie says you were hiding in the toilets. I tried to write you a note in first lesson but you can't get away with anything in Geog – he is dead strict. It's OK now it's Maths. What did you do at the weekend? Did you see Cooper? Did you walk into a wall or something? What's that mark on your face? Signed Katy B **.**

Stop asking me all these QUESTIONS Katy B. Why are you so interested in my life? Who do you think you are, my mum or something? I don't want to talk about it OK? Just pass me our RE homework quick. I'll have to do it during break.

Here's what she gave us for RE homework. I've copied it out for you.

FREE WILL

Christians say that God gave people Free Will so they can make decisions about things. We have a choice, we are not pre-programmed like computers. We can make choices between kindness and cruelty, honesty and dishonesty, selfishness and unselfishness, anger and self-control etc. Write about a time you made a choice like this. Was it the right choice or did you regret it later? Signed *Katy B*.

Oh, Katy, I can't be bothered to think about that. Send me a note quick, tell me something to write.

I dunno Lisa. Write about something that happened in the olden days when you were little. That's always a good move cos choices seemed dead simple then, didn't they? Eg, you got mad with your little sister one day cos she stole your dolly or ate your jelly beans or something so you kicked her teddy bear out the window then you realized you made the WRONG choice and were really sorry afterwards. What about some stuff like that? Signed *Katy B*.

No way. I'm going to write that I wished I'd kicked my sister out of the window as well as her stupid teddy cos then she'd stop stealing my make-up and jewellery and sneaking into my room to look through my things. And if she got kicked out the window I could have her bedroom cos it's bigger than mine and has got more places to plug things in then I could have my hair dryer on as well as my CD and TV.

Don't think they want to hear that, Lisa.
Signed Katy B.

Well, they shouldn't give us such crap homework then should they?

What's wrong with you today? You sound really upset. Why don't you write me a note, tell me what happened between you and Cooper. Maybe there's something I can do.

I said I don't want to talk about it. There's nothing you can do anyway. You can't solve everything, ya know. You're not my Fairy Godmother, ya know. Katy B just waves her magic wand and everything will be all right again like in the fairy stories for little kids. Just mind your own business, Katy. I got to sort this out myself. And stop writing me stupid notes.

FOR J PRESCOTT. PRIVATE!

J, this is Katy B. Do you know what went on between Cooper and Lisa at the weekend? Something's really upset her. She won't even talk to me about it – I'm really worried about her. Have you heard any whispers or have any of Cooper's friends said anything?

Signed Katy B.

I don't hang round with Cooper and his gang. I keep right out of their way. Cos if you get in their way they'll walk right over your face. But I'll see what I can find out. J.

Don't let anyone else see this note. Promise, Katy. Promise U will tear it up into teeny weeny little pieces as soon as you've read it. And whatever U do don't show it to Lisa.

How much are pregnancy tests? Four weeks ago Dexie and me went baby-sitting at my auntie's house and after we put the kids to bed we sort of found some drink at the back of a cupboard. I mean, it was nothing much just cider that's all. So we drank it and we got carried away a bit and I can't remember really what happened but I'm sure we didn't actually do anything but we were fooling around that's all. So I didn't think it mattered. But now I am a week late. I was sure I would start at the weekend but I didn't. I couldn't be pregnant could I, Katy? Not with just messing around like that? I mean we did not even take our clothes off. I couldn't be so unlucky could I, Katy? I am really scared. I don't know what to do. My dad is dead strict and he might throw me out or something. We did not really do it, we were just messing around. You can't get pregnant like that can you Katy? You can't, can you? Not if you don't even take your clothes off? I was trying to think about what we did at school. We had that talk with the nurse, do you remember where we got those free Tampax in a pretty bag with blue daisies on it? And we did about AIDS. And about how babies were born in Biology. But I don't remember anything about just messing about, do you? Are pregnancy tests more than my pocket money? Will you come to town with me Saturday and buy one? I daren't go in for it as my mum knows the lady who serves in the chemist's. Will you ask for it for me? But I don't need one really do I? Not for what we did. Meet me in the girls' toilet at lunch. Now tear this note into tiny pieces like confetti so no one can join it up again. DO NOT TELL NO ONE, not even J and especially not Dexie. Swear! When you get to this bit in the note cross your heart and hope to die. I will be watching to see if you do. Tell me what to do Katy B. You are smart. I'm really desperate. I feel all hot and sick. That isn't because I am pregnant though is it, Katy? It's because I am in a panic. I don't know what to do. My brain won't work properly. It's all scrambled up.

Hi Rachel! Guess who? It's ☺. I want those ear-rings back that you borrowed. You know the ones shaped like little puppy dogs with little bones dangling out their mouths that are really cute and are 9 carat gold that my grandma bought me for Christmas. The little dogs have got real rubies for their eyes you know. I said before that I didn't want them and you could keep them. But I've changed my mind because you're being horrible to me because Dexie kissed me behind the gravestone. I want them back NOW. Your EX best friend. Sophie.

Hi Lisa! This is your friend Sophie☺. Thought I'd better write this note to warn you that Emily is after you. She is really on the warpath! She says that you have been messing Cooper about. She says Ant told her about you flirting with him (and with loads of boys) at the Roller Disco even though Coop warned you not to. I don't know what business it is of hers, do you?

She keeps saying Cooper still likes her but it isn't true. He wouldn't be seen dead with somebody like her. Have you seen her hairstyle from hell? I would put a bag over my head if it was me. And hasn't she heard of Clearasil? She is just jealous of you I expect but I thought you'd like to know. I wouldn't like Emily to be after me. She doesn't care what she does. Remember that time she got mad and punched her fist through the Library door? There was glass all over the place. You had better watch yourself on the school bus. That is where she usually gets people.

She may not do anything of course, she is unpredictable like that. But I thought you'd like to know. What's what friends are for, isn't it? It's a pity I'm going on a different bus tonight or I would back you up if she tried anything.

I can't do this stupid graph. It's going off the page! What is the scale supposed to be? Have you got 10 sq. m every 5 cm or something? Do you know your French vocab. for the test next lesson? I don't – I bet I get 0/10.

PASS TO EMILY STRICTLY PRIVATE

You will be really surprised to get this note. It is Sophie writing it. Yes, Sophie! Hi Emily. Just look up and I'm here, under the poster of the rat's digestive system. I will wave at you. Hi! I am so busy writing Very Important Notes. This is the third one I've written this lesson! Anyway, Emily, you know me, I don't like causing trouble but I thought you'd like to know that Lisa said your hair is like a spiky yellow coconut and that the dye must have gone wrong and that she'd go out with a bag on her head if she was you. She is a bitch sometimes isn't she and really fancies herself? I don't know why as her legs are not that great. They are quite fat at the top. I think she has got cellulite.

I've got some ear-rings you can have if you like. They're really nice. My grandma bought them for me and they are quite valuable with real rubies for eyes but you can have them if you like. You would look nice with two cute little puppy dogs in your ears. They would suit you. They would look really good on you.
Your pal Sophie ☺

Chapter Seven

English

Rach, I'm getting Jonathan to pass you this note so no one else will open it. Don't worry, he does not know anything. Where were you at lunch time? Thought we were supposed to meet in the toilets? I had lots of things to talk to you about. I missed my lunch and went round to see J's mum. She lives just round the corner from school. And I asked her advice as I did not know what to tell you. Don't worry, she does not know who you are, I just said "a friend of mine". I think she thought I might be talking about me and J at first so I had to tell her I was not!

Anyway, she said there is definitely a chance that you might get pregnant with heavy petting but you might be late because you are worrying about it or some other reason. She said you should tell your mum or the school nurse or the doctor as then you will find out for sure. She says it's important to find out as soon as you can and get help. Like counselling

about keeping the baby or adoption or abortion or things like that. I rushed back to school to tell you what she said but you didn't meet me like you said you would Signed Katy B.

What a horrible note. Katy! Why did you ask J's mum? I don't want to think about all those things she said. Anyway, I don't think I need to as I don't think she is right. I don't think there is any chance at all. I told you, we did not really do it we were just on the sofa and we did not even take our clothes off. I wish I hadn't told you now. Why did you ask that woman, she is just trying to frighten me! I cannot tell my mum, she would go mad. You know what she's like, she gets embarrassed even when there are Tampax adverts on the telly. And I don't want to see a doctor or anything or think about all those things you said. It is all too horrible. I hate it, it isn't real anyway so I'm not going to think about it. From NOW.

I don't know – let's you and me go to Boots on Saturday and get a pregnancy test. How much did you say they cost? Will you lend me some money? Will you go in and get it for me in case my mum's friend is serving in there? But what if it is positive – what will I do then? Maybe I will not get a test. I'm so confused. I wish it would all go away. I'm sick of thinking about it. Maybe I will start today. Pottsie asked me a question about Romeo and Juliet just now. Did you hear her? And I just said "What, what?" I didn't even know what she was saying. She said, "Daydreaming again Rachel? Which pop star is it this time?" Look, my hand is shaking when I'm writing this. Dexie said at break, what is the matter with you Rach? Why are you acting so strange? Why are you trying to avoid me?

So did you tell him? Signed *Katy B*.

Course not Katy, do you think I'm stupid?

I haven't spoken about it at all. Not to no one. Not even to you. I can write to you in notes, like this. That is not so bad somehow. But I can't talk about it. When I try the words won't come out my mouth.

Rach, I think you should speak to someone before Saturday. You have to TALK about it. You can't just keep on writing me notes forever.

Careful when you pass your answer back. Pass it under the desk. Pottsie nearly caught me last time. Signed *Katy B*.

Will you stop nagging me Katy B? You are as bad as my mum. You are only making it worse. Friends should not do that – they should make things better. They should say, "Don't worry Rach.

Everything will be all right!" Anyway, I am not worried. I've decided not to think about it any more OK? I'll think about it Saturday. So we won't write any more notes about it. If you write me one I won't open it. I'll tear it up in little bits and throw it away. I'm not thinking about it from

Chapter Eight

Library

Hi! It's guess who? It's ☺! Will you do me a big favour Katy B? I'm doing this questionnaire called How Popular Are You? from my magazine but Question 5 says "Get someone to fill this in for you." So I thought, "Katy B will do it, she is one of my best friends." I have torn out the question so will you fill in the answer and pass it straight back so I can add up my score? I have scored all a)s so far which means I am very popular but I do not mind if you put a ring round the c). Just be honest, OK?

I hate private study in the library, don't you? You can't even talk. I'm supposed to be looking up "the most important export of New Zealand" for geography but there isn't a book about it. Do you know where one is? This is a rubbish library isn't it?

PASS TO SOPHIE

Sophie, here is your questionnaire back.

Signed Katy B.

When Sophie is absent from school do you:
a) rush round after school to give her the latest gossip
b) phone her in the evening – if you've nothing better to do
(c) say, when she returns, "So how long have you been off then?"

Lisa, Hi, this is guess who? ☺ I had to choose a friend to fill in this questionnaire about how popular I am so naturally I thought of you first. Just be honest, OK? I am sorry it is a bit smeary as I have been rubbing out some pencil marks on it. Did Emily do anything on the bus last night? She is a cow, isn't she. I mean, who does she think she is? It is none of her business whether you two-timed Cooper or not. Actually, didn't you four-time him as I saw you dancing with three boys?

FOR SOPHIE

When *Sophie* is absent from school do you:

a) rush round after school to give her the latest gossip

b) phone her in the evening – if you've nothing better to do

(c) say, when she returns, "So how long have you been off then?"

I have filled in your questionnaire. I'm sending it back. I did not four-time Cooper. How do you work that out? I just danced with some boys at the Roller Disco, that's all. What's wrong with that? I didn't even meet them afterwards or anything. But Cooper got to hear about it somehow. Anyway, I don't have anything to do with Cooper now. Last night I told him I wanted to finish him. So that is all over and done with. I have got rid of him for good.

Emily didn't do anything on the bus last night cos I was not on the bus. After you told me she was after me I walked home. I took a short cut through the industrial estate and across the park.

FOR EMILY. VERY URGENT!!!

Yes it's me ☺ writing VIN (Very Important Notes) again. It's such a drag, being so popular. Anyway, guess what? Lisa just told me that she has finished with Cooper! Who does she think she is? Coop will not like that, will he? Nobody finishes with Cooper. She's asking for trouble if you ask me. And guess what again? She said she didn't go home on the school bus yesterday. Don't ask me why. She walked home instead. I bet she does the same thing tonight. It must be miles the way she goes, you know, up the High Street and then right down Morrison Avenue and then through the industrial estate and across the park where it is all lonely and no one could see if she got beat up or something. Here is a map, in case you don't know the way she is going.

Anyway, if you ask me I think Miss Popular is cracking up. Just take a look at her. Go on, take a sneaky look now. She is sitting by Fiction A to E. She looks a mess – her hair is all greasy. When did she last wash it? And it's no good plastering make-up on, you can still see that big fat zit on her chin. Don't know why people think she's so pretty. I never did.

Do not bother to write a note back. I won't mind because I know you don't like school and writing and homework and stuff. I don't blame you one bit. It is really boring!

FOR RACHEL. STRICTLY PRIVATE
Rach, it's Katy B. Look, I know you said you didn't want to think about it until Saturday but do you want to come with me to talk to J's mum tomorrow lunch time? She is a really nice person, honest. She understands things. Nobody will know. It will still be a secret. You can trust her. She will not tell anyone, even J. But you need to TALK to someone and maybe it would be easier with a stranger.

NO NO NO NO NO NO NO NO NO NO NO NO! LEAVE ME ALONE KATY B! You are just trying to scare me. I wish I had never told you now.

Katy, this is J. Haven't found out much about what happened between Lisa and Cooper. Except he's been calling her all sorts of awful names like slut and slag and whispering things about her with his mates. Then they all burst out laughing. And I heard him talking to Ant, something about her failing a test. What's that mean? My mum says to come round tonight if you like, she will cook spaghetti. You got your copy of To Kill a Mockingbird with you? Pass it over if you have. I've got to read Chapter 4 before English.

Nearly forgot, the Belgian hare had three babies last night. One was too weak. It died even though me and Mum wrapped it up in a towel, tried everything we could to keep it alive. I stayed up all night with it but it died four o'clock this morning just as the sun was coming up. The other two are strong though. If you want to, you could choose one of them to keep for yourself when they're old enough. Except I think you said your mum won't let you have pets because they are too messy or spread germs or something. J.

Please Lisa, I know you said mind my own business and not try to be your Fairy Godmother and not write you notes or anything but please, please tell me what is going on between you and Cooper. It is a good chance to write me a note now, in Library lesson. Have you finished with him or what? I am supposed to be

your best friend but you've hardly spoken to me lately. Signed Katy B.

Katy, I am only writing this because Cooper and Ant are in Technology. Tear this note up after you've read it. Tear it into little tiny pieces and throw it away so Cooper can't find it and stick it back together again. If he knew I was writing about him to you he would go crazy. I'm really scared, Katy. I thought I could handle all this but I can't. Cooper is like a different person. He was nice to me before and good-looking and good fun to be with. But he's changed into someone horrible. I can't believe it – it's like some kind of nightmare. He went mad after the Roller Disco. He said I was flirting with other boys and I said I wasn't and I said "How do you know?" And he said, "I've got my spies. I'm watching you all the time even when I'm not there. I know everything you do." When I tried to argue with him he pushed me and I fell over and that's how I got this bruise on my face. But he wasn't sorry, he just said it served me right. I suppose it did in a way – I shouldn't have danced with those boys, should I? I should have done what Cooper said. I suppose it was all my fault really.

Are you as crazy as him Lisa? How can it be your fault? How can you say that? You stay away from him. Do not have anything to do with him. How dare he push you

like that? I should've warned you before. I mean, there were warning signs weren't there, with the matches and the knife and all those stupid tests he kept setting you? Don't know why I didn't see it, more clearly. But I'm telling you now, someone like him is nothing but bad news like J said. He's dangerous. Keep away from him. Please. Signed Katy B.

That's easy to say, Katy, but what am I supposed to do? He won't leave me alone. He is calling me names all the time. He even phoned up my house last night and shouted names down the phone. It's like he's gone crazy. He says he will tell people horrible things about me, about things that we never did. I told him I had finished with him again over the phone. I said, "I don't want anything to do with you." But he said, "You don't think it's that easy do you? You're not going to escape as easy as that." And, as well as him, Sophie says that Emily is after me. Sophie says that Emily is going to wait for me tonight and beat me up. It must be true because look at Emily now, she is staring at me and giving me dirty looks. I cannot stand it, all these people hating me. Even Cooper's mates are sniggering about me now. I wish I had never met him! Do not forget, tear this note up. Make certain it is totally destroyed else he will find it. I know he will. Wish I could fly. Wish I had great big feathery wings like angels so I could fly away to somewhere where Cooper couldn't find me.

PASS TO EMILY. READ THIS NOTE NOW!
Emily, you'd better answer this note. It's from Katy B. I know you act tough and everyone says you are the toughest girl in our year and the best fighter. But I'm not scared of you. See? Lisa's my best friend and I look after her so you'd better not lay a finger on her because if you do you'll answer to me. See? Just because you are jealous of her and Cooper. It is not your business who she goes out with and anyway, she is not going out with him any more. She has finished him. Remember what I said – you keep away from Lisa. She has got friends to protect her. Write me an answer NOW to tell me you'll leave her alone.

What are you talking about? Who's told you that I'm after Lisa? I couldn't care less about her. I'm not interested in her. I'm not interested in Cooper either. He is a bastard. And I'm not jealous. I'm glad he's going out with her. It means that he can be a bastard to someone else now and not threaten me all the time. Your friend Lisa is a little fool anyway. She made a big mistake trying to finish him.

She should have done the same as me. Soon as I found out what he is really like, I got out of it by making him finish me. It was easy, I just made sure he saw me smoking and he finished me straight away. Cooper is dead strict about smoking, he hates girls smoking. Do not write me no more notes, I don't like them. They are stupid – all scheming and secret and sneaky. You want to ask me something just shout across the classroom and I will shout my answer back to you. Simple as that. What's the use of passing all these notes around?

Lisa, one good bit of news. I'll write quick cos the lesson's nearly over. EMILY IS NOT AFTER YOU. She has just told me in a note. She says she's not interested in you. She's just pleased to get away from Cooper. She says you should not have tried to finish him. You should have got him to finish you. Signed Katy B.

What do you think I was trying to do at the Roller Disco? I'm not stupid Katy B, even though you seem to think I am. Even before the disco I didn't like him any more. He is good-looking and tough and at first he was nice. But he's really creepy as well. He made me scared with all those things he did with the matches and the knife although I didn't tell you. Remember you liked him as well at first. You thought he was a good catch! Anyway, I thought if I flirted with loads of other boys at the disco he would finish me. But everything went wrong he did not finish me he just went berserk so I had to finish him and he said, "No girl ever finishes me" and now he is going to make me pay for what I did.

Hi Katy B! ☺ You are so smart so why haven't you answered my question about the most important export of New Zealand? I sent you a note about it at the beginning of this Library lesson and it is the end now and you still haven't sent me a note even though I've seen you writing notes to loads of other people. Don't you like me any more or something? Even if you don't like me and even though you chose c) in the questionnaire I will still be your friend.
PS. You wouldn't like some ear-rings like little gold puppy dogs with real rubies for eyes would you? They are 9 carat gold and quite valuable. Silly me, I forgot, you do not have your ears pierced do you? But I would give them to you if you had.

Chapter Nine

Maths

PASS TO J PRESCOTT. URGENT!

J, have you seen Lisa in school today? She was not in games this morning. She was supposed to be my partner at badminton but she didn't turn up. I'm getting really worried. Send me a note back, quick. Signed Katy B.

No, I haven't seen her. Cooper asked where she was. He was looking all round the school for her. He was really angry that he couldn't find her.

I can't concentrate on this maths. I'm too worried about Lisa to think straight. How do you find the curved surface area of a cone anyway? I've forgotten what you do. Look at what I found in the back of Lisa's copy of To Kill a Mockingbird that she lent to me because I lent

mine to you before last English lesson and you never gave it back.

July 10th, 2.25 am. LAST WILL AND TESTAMENT OF LISA HUTCHINSON

I want my sister to have my clothes as she is always borrowing them anyway. Any that she does not like I want to be given to Oxfam so they can send them to orphans in Bosnia or somewhere. But I want Katy B to have my white silk shirt with the pearly buttons as she has always liked it and she does not get much money for clothes.

Rachel can have my collection of teddy bears except for the tiny one called Pudsey with the red ribbon round his neck. My mum can keep him. It will remind her of me. And my sister can have my jewellery except for my gold chain with the St Christopher on it. Daniel Stephenson in 10Y can have that as he was kind and I liked him best of all the boys I went out with even though I did finish him. Tell him that I always liked him best.

Katy B, in the top drawer of my bedside table there is a five year diary. The key is hidden in that little straw basket on my bookcase under the soaps shaped like shells. You can read it if you like. I am sorry for all the times I was a bitch to you. I couldn't help it but you were always my best friend really. You've looked after me since I was little.

I want Love Lifts Us Up Where We Belong to be played at my funeral as it's my mum's favourite. And all my friends can choose their favourite song to be played at my funeral. No flowers. And nobody must cry or wear black.

I am not scared any more. I feel like this is the only way I can escape and anyway I will see Grandma and Grandad again.

Love you all

Bye, bye, especially to Katy B.

From Lisa.

Isn't that really sad J? You don't think she means it, do you? You don't think she might do something stupid do you? I mean she was depressed about Cooper always checking up on her, never leaving her alone, but I never thought she would go this far. Should I show this to someone? Should I show it to her mum? Signed Katy B.

PASS TO KATY B
9xrxl

What's that mean, Jonathan? That note you just sent? Signed Katy B.

It's how to find the surface area of that cone. You asked me about it didn't you? J

J, are you crazy! I don't care about stupid cones! I've just passed you Lisa's will where she talks about her funeral and she says "no flowers" and stuff. I want to know what we're going to do about it? The more I think about it the more worried I get. See that bit where she says, "Send my clothes to orphans in Bosnia"? She always was kind and thoughtful like that. Signed Katy B.

Give me a chance, Katy. I'm just reading it. I'm a slow reader. J.

PASS TO KATY B. STRICTLY PRIVATE!

Katy, U will not believe it. I have got some wonderful news for U. I am not pregnant. I'll write it again. I AM NOT PREGNANT! I looked for U at break to tell U but I couldn't find U. I started last night. I feel like I am free again, like dancing round the room and yelling it out to everyone but of course I can't as it is a secret and I didn't tell anyone but U. U didn't tell anyone else did U, cross your heart and hope to die? Wasn't I stupid for worrying like that? I'm ashamed of myself now. I got U all worked up and

U needn't have bothered to go and see J's mum for me. That was a waste of time anyway as she was only trying to scare me.

It's GREAT though isn't it? I'm going to go out to celebrate with Dexie tonight even though he won't know what we are celebrating. I'm HAPPY HAPPY HAPPY. Life is WONDERFUL. Yes! Look at me and I'll give you a big grin. I'm smiling all over my face. I can't stop, I just can't stop. My face is aching I'm grinning so much and in a maths lesson too – Mr Spenser will think I've gone crazy. He'll think I like maths! You've got to promise not to tell Dexie about any of this. I just want to forget about it now. It is all over and done with. Honest Katy, it was the worst time of my life and I just want to forget it.

Your news is great Rach. It's a big relief and I'm really happy for you and everything. But you and Dexie had better watch out in the future. And you'd better keep off the drink or you could be in trouble for real next time. Signed Katy B.

Katy B, trust U, U R a real spoilsport! I don't want to think about gloomy things now. Why do U always see the serious side of things when everything is all right? I'll think about all that later, honest I will. I just don't want to think about it now. Just be happy 4 me, OK? When I smile at U give me a big smile back. Go on, it won't hurt U! And relax. Wave! Hiya Rach! It's been terrible these last few days, U do not know what it's been like and I just want to be happy now. I don't want to be reminded of when I was miserable so do not do it, U are supposed to be my friend so do not upset me. Right?

I can't concentrate on these maths at all. Who cares about the surface area of a cone? I don't care about that, do U? What has that got to do with anything? Do you ever have to do it in real life?

Guess what? My horoscope said yesterday that there was a big surprise in my stars and it has turned out to be true! So just be happy 4 me, OK? And please, please, please don't preach at me Katy B and make me feel miserable again.

FOR KATY B

This is J. See what you mean about being worried. Just finished reading Lisa's will. Took me ages cos Spenser kept prowling round our table and I had to look as if I was working out these cones. But he's gone now. Does anyone else know where Lisa is? What about Rachel or Sophie?

Maybe the will is just a joke or something. J.

J, how can you say it's a joke? Haven't you got any feelings? It made me cry just reading it. It's really serious! Signed Katy B.

We've got to find her then. Maybe Cooper's found her by now. Shall I ask him at break if he knows where she is? J

OK but be careful. Cooper is really unpredictable. He doesn't like you anyway and he might think you're interfering or after Lisa yourself or something. Watch your step. Try and get him on his own. He's worse when he's got a crowd of friends round him, got to prove he's a hard man all the time. I'll pass a note to Rachel when Spenser stops pacing about and goes back to his desk. I'll ask her if she's seen Lisa. Signed Katy B.

PASS TO RACHEL. URGENT
Rach, this is Katy. Do you know why Lisa isn't at school today? Write me a note straight back. Be careful though, pass it under the table. Spenser's giving me the evil eye. Signed Katy B.

Don't ask me where she is. I've hardly spoken to her lately. And stop worrying, be cool like I am. Spenser won't see nothing. He's blind as a bat in those new contact lenses. Guess what, that little bitch Sophie is still causing trouble between me and Dexie. Can U believe it? Honestly, I hate her. She's got these big blue eyes like a Barbie doll and acts all sweet and nice. The teachers just love her. But underneath she's a real schemer, a real trouble maker. I think she's trying to split me and Dexie up. Well, she is not having him! Do U know what she did? She wrote, "Rachel loves Graham, True," on my pencil case when I wasn't looking. She put it on a little heart with an arrow through it like this:

U know who Graham is? He's that boy I used to go out with ages ago with red hair and freckles and big teeth in 10R – I wouldn't be seen dead with him now. But if Dexie saw that on my pencil case he would go mad and think I still like Graham. But I saw it in time and rubbed it off. Do U think Sophie is really trying to get Dexie off me? Is 22.5 metres the answer to number 5 and can I borrow your pencil sharpener shaped like a banana?

Rach, you dummy, don't you ever think about anything but yourself? I don't care about Sophie and her stupid little schemes. This is serious. I asked you in my note where Lisa was. She's in real trouble. She needs my help. Signed Katy B.

Sorree! U didn't tell me it was Life and Death, Katy. Why didn't U say so? I will ask around but it is funny cos even though Lisa was dead popular she did not have many real friends did she? U are the only one left who cares a lot. Except me – I care a lot of course. But some people only pretended 2 like her – they were jealous of her really. Because she was so gorgeous looking and she never even had spots and no problems getting boys. And her hair was so blonde and shiny and never greasy. How did she get it like that, mine always goes greasy? Anyway, these people who only pretended 2 like her, they're the ones that are saying she got what she deserved with Cooper. They say she thought she was Miss Perfect, looked down her nose at everyone. Thought she was better than anyone else. They say she was silly and spoiled and vain and needed teaching a lesson. Of course, I don't say things like that. It's just that I've HEARD some other people saying them. I will ask around as soon as I've sent that bitch Sophie a note. But what I'm saying is, I don't think anyone but U much cares where Lisa is.

FOR THAT BITCH SOPHIE

Keep your hands off Dexie if U want to keep breathing! He is mine. We've been going out, like FOREVER. U know who this is from.

PS. This is just a friendly warning.

Hi! What are you talking about, Rachel Nixon? I have no idea what you mean! Have you gone soft in the head or something? I would not fancy Simon Dexter if he was the last boy left in this school, in the world, in the galaxy, in the universe even. Sophie ☺

J, it's terrible. Everyone but us is deserting Lisa. Even Rachel doesn't care about her now. I know Lisa's selfish sometimes and hurts people. But she isn't like that really. It's just being thoughtless – most of the time she doesn't even realize what she's doing. She's kind really. They don't know her like I do. She can't help being like she is. Her dad calls her Princess and her mum is dead proud of her getting lots of boyfriends and being so pretty. See, Lisa's used to people being nice to her and getting what she wants. She's led a sort of charmed life. So it's not her fault, is it, that she can't cope when things go wrong. She has never had to do that, she hasn't had any practice. She's useless at it. She needs looking after. She needs all the help she can get. Signed Katy B.

Don't think anyone could cope with Cooper no matter how much practice they'd had. I think she needs all the help she can get too. I'll ask Cooper at break if he knows where she is. I'm psyching myself up to it. Wish me luck. J.

PASS TO DEXIE

Dexie, do U fancy Sophie? Tell me straight. Just write YES or NO on this piece of paper and I will understand.

Rachel xxxxx

NO!

Just NO? What kind of an answer is that? U R not being straight with me Simon Dexter. U do fancy her, don't U?

Chapter Ten
French

FOR KATY B

Katy, this is J. Had to play volleyball at lunch time, didn't get the chance to tell you what happened when I saw Cooper. It's a bad idea writing this in French lesson. She could see a flea spit. I'll go out the front, get the big dictionary, drop this on your desk when I go past.

Hier comme petit déjeuner j'ai mangé un paquet de—

Had to write that, she came snooping round to see what I was doing. How do you say "prawn cocktail crisps" in French?

So I go up to Cooper, right? I say, "Can I have a word?" So he just stares at me like I was something he scraped off his Doc Martens. You know the way he stares – little robot eyes like that shark in *Jaws*. He doesn't even blink. How's he do that, not blink? So after he's flexed his pecs for a bit and made me squirm wondering if he's going to get me in a headlock, he says, "So what's your problem?" And while he's saying it he's smirking round at his mates because I tried to get him on his own but I couldn't. He's hardly ever on his own.

et comme déjeuner j'ai mangé deux saucissons et un sandwich H.P. sauce

God, she nearly copped me that time!

So I say to Cooper (you'd be proud of me, Katy B, my voice didn't even tremble – much) "You know where Lisa is? Her friends want to know. They think she might be in trouble." So he says, like a gangsta, "What business is it of yours, creep? Lisa's my business. You trying to interfere in my business?" And his eyes are going wild, you know, the way they do and I'm thinking he's about to break every bone in my body and the crowd around him goes dead quiet like they're just waiting for it to happen, sort of licking their lips and just waiting. But then Cooper laughs and shrugs like I'm not worth the effort and everyone else laughs as well and I can see he's not going to hit me. Instead he says, very quiet with one hand on my shoulder, like he's giving me some friendly advice, "You leave Lisa to me. OK? Leave me to worry about her. If she's in trouble I'll know about it. I'll fix it. And I don't want no one else interfering. She's my business now. You understand?"

And he's talking and smiling but all the time his hand is gripping tighter and tighter on my shoulder. And I'm trying not to show it but it hurts like hell and I'm almost crying out with the pain cos his hands are very strong, he lifts weights. And his fingers are digging into my shoulder muscles but nobody knows that but me and him. They're all amazed he hasn't bounced me off the walls yet. They think I'm really lucky cos he must be in a good mood and being really tolerant.

Then he stares into my eyes just once. This sort of killer's stare. Then he lets me go and turns his back on me. Starts laughing and talking with his mates as if I don't exist or I'm a microbe or something, like invisible to the human eye.

Then when I get changed for volleyball someone says, "What's that on your shoulder?" And I take a look and there are five red marks, where Cooper's fingers have dug in.

So that's it. Waste of time. I didn't find out whether he knows where Lisa is or not. It's impossible to tell what he's thinking. Did you already check her house? Maybe there's nothing to worry about, maybe she's just at home sick or something.

Can you come round to my house Saturday? The baby rabbits have got their eyes open now.

I already rang Lisa's house. Rang at lunchtime from the payphone. She's not there. Or she's not answering the phone. I'll try again after school.

Too risky writing notes in French – she's on the prowl again. She catches you, you have to learn 50 irregular verbs – all tenses! Fate worse than death.

Katy B.

Chapter 11
Morning Assembly

All things bright and beautiful
All creatures great and small
All things wise and wonderful
The Lord God made them all.

PASS TO KATY B

Lisa's back. Look round now, the row behind me, sharing hymn books with Rach. Seems fine to me – now maybe you'll stop worrying about her. Look, you coming round Saturday or what? Got a cross country run after this assembly. Up heart attack hill in this pouring rain. Talk about sadism. See you at break – if I live that long. Might need mouth to mouth resus. when I get back. You available? J.

The purple-headed mountain
The river running by
The sunset and the morning
That brightens up the sky.

PASS TO PRESCOTT

Looks OK doesn't she? She's even singing! Girls' PE been cancelled. Leaky roof in the gym or something. We've got "supervised private study" next. Can't wait to write her a note, find out what's going on. Won't see you at break – me and Lisa have got lots to talk about.

Signed Katy B.

Chapter Twelve

Private Study

Lisa! Great to see you. I was worried sick about you. Phoned your house yesterday and let it ring for ages but there was no answer. So where were you? Write me a note straight back. Katy B.

What's all the fuss about? You're always checking up on me, Katy B. You're worse than my mum! Just felt like staying at home, didn't I? Didn't want to talk to ANYONE – so I never answered the phone. That's no big deal is it?

Who's this freak supervising us? Is he a supply teacher or what? Look at those white socks and sandals. Yuk. He must have a death wish. He's useless. He won't last the day, I bet. Wait till 10Y get hold of him, they'll crucify him. Look, I'm not even hiding this note. I'm writing it right under his nose and he daren't do nothing about it.

But what about you and Cooper? And I found something in the back of your "To Kill a Mocking Bird". It

was a will, Lisa, don't say it wasn't. You left your clothes to orphans and your diary to me and you said, "I want to be cremated and no flowers." Honest, I was sick with worry. I was worried you might do something stupid. Just write me the truth. Write me it NOW, OK? Don't be scared Cooper'll see it. Or Ant. They're out running up heart attack hill.

Oh, so you found the will did you? Can't keep any secrets from you Katy, can I? OK so I was a bit depressed when I wrote that. But I didn't mean it. It was just sort of experimenting, thinking how guilty you'd all feel if I did really truly kill myself and how you'd all cry like mad at the funeral. Even Emily. And how sad you'd all be. I even thought of ways to do it. But that's all over now. And so what if Cooper sees what I'm writing. I don't care. It's all sorted out between me and him. He isn't being horrible to me any more.

You know that shirt I promised you in my will with the pearly buttons? Well, you can still have it even though I'm not going to kill myself. Have it as a present.

Lisa, I'm all confused. Is that psycho Cooper really leaving you alone? That's great. But how did it happen? Write me a note quick and tell me.
PS. It's OK about the shirt you keep it. Katy B.

Don't you call Coop a psycho, Katy. Deep down he's a really nice boy. And I never said he'd left me alone, did I? Because he called me last night. At least he didn't or I'd have hung up on him. But Ant called and he handed over the phone to Coop before I knew what he was doing. And Coop said, "Please don't hang up." And honestly Katy, he was like a totally different person. He didn't threaten me once or call me a slag. He was like he was at first, you know, soooo charming and saying nice things all the time. Mr Romantic. We were on the phone for ages and Katy, he knows what a bastard he's been! He said he'll change. That he's DEFINITELY learned his lesson. And I think he really means it. He begged me to go back to him. He says, "You can't see me but I'm down on my knees. Aren't I down on my knees, Ant? You tell her." And Ant takes the phone and says, "Believe me, he really is. I've never seen him like this before. What have you done to the guy? He must be really in love. He's really got it bad."

Then he hands the phone back and Cooper begs, "Just give me another chance. I'll treat you right, I promise I will. I don't want to lose you, Lisa." What do you think about that, Katy B? Can you believe it? Coop was on his knees and begging? And I forgot, he said, "I never beg for anything Lisa. But I'm begging for you. That's how much you've changed me." I feel quite sorry for him!

Lisa! This is serious now. OK? I'm writing seriously to you now so stop painting your nails. You didn't say you'd meet him again did you? You didn't fall for all that junk he said over the phone? I'm not trying to tell you what to do or anything but stay away from him Lisa. Just run a mile. He's trouble. Promise me you'll do what I tell you. PROMISE! Let me see you cross your heart and hope to die.

TO KATY B AIRMAIL!

See that, Katy B? Chrissie Parker made a note into a dart and chucked it at Rachel and it flew right past his ear and he never even looked up. But he knows what's going on, look, his ears are red like two cherries. Hey, there's bits of paper zooming all over the place, it's a snowstorm! I'm going to fold this up when I've finished and colour it with my felt-tips so it's a beautiful butterfly to fly to you, one of my bestest friends.

This is me, Sophie ☺ by the way. And what I'm writing this note for is this: RACH AND DEXIE HAVE BROKEN UP. Yes they have! Didn't you know? Everyone's talking about it because they've been going out, like FOREVER. If you ask me she got too serious acting like she owned him and he got sick of it.

Well, I will not treat him like that. And by the way,

that's the number 2 reason I'm writing this note. Will you do me a MASSIVE favour, Katy B? Will you ask DEXIE (DEXIE SOPHIE) if he wants to go out with ME? I know he fancies me because he chased me round the computer suite once. You ask him because that's what friends are for and I'm too shy with boys.

Only, do you think it's too soon to ask him as he only broke up with Rachel before morning assembly?

PASS TO EMILY STRICTLY CONFIDENTIAL

You'll get a surprise when you unfold this plane. It's a note from Katy B. I know you think passing notes is for wimps but this is too private to shout across the classroom. I want you to do something. Lisa has just written me a note. She says Cooper wants her back. She says he's begged her ON HIS KNEES (can you believe that?) to give him another chance. He's told her he's changed and she believes him! I want you to back me up. Write her a note. Tell her he's really dangerous, tell her what he's really like. She might listen to you. So will you do it? Just write your answer on this plane and fly it back to me.

Why should I? Why should I help Lisa out? We've been four years in the same class and she's hardly spoken to me once. Why should I help either of you? Both of you think you're better than me, don't you? You think I'm thick and Miss Perfect thinks I'm trash. Your plane flies lousy. I'm going to re-design it. Make it aerodynamic.

Wouldn't ask for your help if I thought you were thick, would I? I'm just scared of you, that's all. I keep out of your way.

Yeah well, I can understand that. Cos people like you and Miss Perfect generally make me sick. Anyhow what you so worried about her for? She wouldn't worry about you if you were in trouble. Let her sort out her own problems. You can always pick up the pieces afterwards.

Can't do that. I'm Lisa's best friend, aren't I? She depends on me, ever since toddler group. I've got responsibilities. What am I supposed to do, just stand by and watch her wreck her life?

Her choice, isn't it? She's not a toddler no more. She's grown up. There's no more space on this plane. Send me a fresh one. Only make it fly straight this time.

What do you mean her choice? She's trapped good and proper. If she doesn't meet Cooper he'll make her life hell. If she does meet him he'll make her life hell. What kind of a choice is that?

Hey, Katy B, maybe Cooper's really changed. Maybe it's a miracle and he's turned into a kind and caring person. You thought about that?

Don't joke, Emily. This is dead serious.

How can I take it serious? What have Miss Perfect's problems been before now? Running out of lip gloss. Tragic! Breaking a nail. Like, major disaster! How can you take anyone like her serious? She's so dumb, it's pathetic. She deserves what she gets. You can scrap this plane now. Its wing's bent and I'm not writing no more stupid notes on it.

Just one last note. Lisa's not like you think she is. You don't know her like I do. There must be some way I can get her out of this mess.

Not if she doesn't want your help there isn't.

Chapter Thirteen
Maths

Hi Katy B! Stop doing that boring old Maths and read this note. Cooper gave me a card yesterday. Look up NOW and I'll hold it up quick so you can see it. Actually Coop didn't give it to me personally – he sent Ant to give it to me cos he was probably too embarrassed. I love that cute little mouse on the front, don't you, with the basket of flowers. And inside he's written, "Please give me another chance, Lisa. Please say you'll meet me Saturday." Isn't that sweet? Specially since it was my fault as well. I did make him mad by dancing with those other boys at the Roller Disco. He's drawn a heart broken into two pieces. Awwww! I feel sorry for him now!

Just spied your little pal J out of the window, coming up the drive. He's late into school isn't he? Naughty boy.

So anyhow Katy B, don't you dare say Cooper hasn't changed. You apologize for calling him a psycho. I know him better than you do. He acts hard but inside he's not really. He's quite soft and squishy! He's kind to animals, did you know that? Once I was with him and we saw a stray kitten and he was really gentle with it. You should have seen him, Katy B. He wrapped it up in his coat and talked to it in baby talk. Someone like that can't be all that bad can they? And he hasn't said one single horrible thing about me since I said I'd think about going back with him.

PASS TO LISA. PRIVATE

He's just playing some kind of game, Lisa, why can't you see that? Once he gets you back he'll be just like he was before. I bet him and Ant laughed themselves silly when they were writing that card. And what kind of a reason is that to go back to him – just so he stops calling you names and spreading lies about you?

It isn't just that. The thing is, if he really changed, if he was nice to me, I'd really like him. If only he'd be nice – cos a lot of the time he's dead charming, you know, and like, good fun to be with.

Yeah, as long as you do exactly what he says. Come on Lisa, grow up. He's got you all mixed up. Can't you see he's bad news. Say no. Say that you've definitely finished with him. He'll call you names for a while. But it

can't go on forever can it? He'll get bored after a while, won't he? He'll just give up and it'll be all over.

No, it's not that easy. He won't give up Katy. You don't know Cooper. He won't stop, ever. If I don't go back he won't ever leave me alone.

Stop writing me notes. Stop telling me what to do. You're just confusing me. I got to finish this Maths. I'm in big trouble already with Mr Spenser for not doing my homework.

You're scared of Cooper, aren't you, Lisa? He's got you scared out of your mind. That's why you're going back to him.

Oh shut up, Katy B. You don't know what you're talking about. You always think you know what's going on inside my head but you don't. Nobody does but me. And I am grown up – I don't need you to take care of me all the time. I can take care of myself. Why don't you mind your own business? Why don't you write notes to your little chum J Prescott? He's just come into class and you never even noticed. He looks terrible – like he's seen a ghost.

PASS TO JONATHAN PRESCOTT

This is Katy. Where were you at registration? Did you miss the bus? You look dreadful. Are you sick or something? Why are your eyes all red? Here's the answers to questions 1 and 2 on the worksheet so you can catch up.

1. 27.9m

2. 5.78m

PASS TO KATY B

He killed my Belgian hares, Katy. Cooper did it. He climbed over our garden wall last night and broke the padlock on the cage door and snapped their necks. He dragged the doe out and snapped her neck and he bashed the babies' brains out on the garden wall. I found them like that this morning when I went to feed them. There was blood and mess all over the place, I threw up when I found them. Didn't want my mum to see them like that. That's why I was late – I dug a hole in the back garden, buried them so she wouldn't have to see them when she went outside to hang up the washing or something.

That's awful J. That's terrible. I can't believe it. I mean, not even Cooper— Did you see him? Are you sure it was him? Did he leave a note or something?

Didn't need to leave a note did he? I got the message. Stop interfering in Cooper's business or it'll be your neck next. Your blood on the wall. That was the message.

You saying it wasn't him? Course it was him! I didn't see him but I know it was him. It's just the kind of thing he'd do. He dragged her out, snapped her neck. He could do that easy, like clicking his fingers. And I bet he never thought twice about it, it didn't bother him at all.

And I never even heard, I never did a thing to save them. I just slept right through it. I know Cooper. He did it to teach me a lesson. That's the way he operates. He thought I was getting right out of order, asking him questions about your friend Lisa.

Look J, here's the answer to no 3 as well.
3. 102m.
I don't know what else to write J. Except I'm really sorry, getting you involved in all of this. I'm really sorry about the Belgian hares. I don't know what else to say.

Nothing to say, is there? Except that I hate him so much that my brain feels like it's going to burst. Except that I'm definitely going to kill him.

Come on J, don't be stupid. You must have a death wish. You must be suicidal. No one goes up against Cooper. No one. You can't win. Look, I know you're really upset but please don't do anything crazy. You can't even prove it was him. Besides, Lisa said something about him being kind to animals, about him taking care of stray kittens or something.

Oh yeah, what are you, a big fan of his or something? And I suppose he helps little old ladies across the street? Suppose Lisa told you that as well. I'm sick of hearing about Lisa. Lisa Lisa Lisa, don't you ever think about no one else?

I know it was him, no question. And I'm going to get him. So don't write me any more notes. I got to do this Maths.

And anyhow there's nothing else to write.

Katy B, this is from guess who? ☺ Yes, it's me. You couldn't do me a meganormous favour could you? Well, you know that note I sent you yesterday about Dexter and Rachel splitting up before morning assembly and me asking you to ask Dexie to meet me but then wondering if it was too soon to ask him? Well, he has had a whole day to get over his broken heart 💔 so will you ask him for me NOW please,

please, please pretty please. Only I don't want to wait too long or someone else might grab him.

Stop pestering me with your stupid notes Sophie you slimy little creep. I've got more important things to think about than your pathetic love life.

Lisa! This is your friend ☺ Sophie. I'm ever so upset. I have just got a very rude, bad-tempered note from Katy B. I was shocked! I thought she was Miss Cool! What is the matter with her today? Did she get out the wrong side of bed or something? Is she in a bad mood or something? If she is not careful I will stop being friends with her and I will not write her a note ever again!

Anyway, she will not ask Dexie to meet me. I bet it is cos she secretly fancies him herself! So will you write him a note and ask him for me quick before she gets him. You are a much better friend than grouchy old Katy B. You don't even have to write the note, look, I've written it for you. It is inside this note, have you found it? Just pass it to Dexie, that's SIMON DEXTER, so it looks as if it comes from you and not from me. I don't want it to look like I'm too keen because all the magazines say you should play hard to get.

Dear Dexie. Do you want to meet Sophie ☺? She has asked me (Lisa, hi!) to ask you for her as she is soooo shy with boys. She is a really popular girl and lots of boys fancy her like mad. But she says she likes you better than the rest. Lucky you.

PASS TO LISA

NO NO NO NO NO NO NO NO. How many times have I got to write NO? I would not meet her if there was only me and her left alive after a nuclear holocaust! If all human beings were wiped out by hostile alien life forms from the planet Zarg and there was only me and her left I would not meet her. Tell her that I cannot stand her, that I have never been able to stand her and even if she offered me a zillion trillion squillion pounds I still WOULD NOT MEET HER. Have I made myself perfectly clear?

Sophie this is Lisa. I have sent Dexie your note like you asked me to and he's sent me an answer straight back. I might be wrong but something tells me he is not all that interested in going out with you. I expect it is nothing personal. It is just too soon after Rachel.

I don't think you asked him properly Lisa. I will get someone else to ask him who will ask him properly. He does not mean no, he is just shy. Lots of boys are shy with me – they just need persuading.

THIS IS FOR LISA.
ANYONE ELSE READS THIS NOTE THEY'RE DEAD
Katy B asked me to write you a note and at first I told her to get lost and that it was a total waste of my time. But you're being so stupid that someone's got to give you some advice. So here it is. You crazy or something girl? Cooper is a natural-born bastard. If you think he'll change for you you're crazy. If you think you can change him you're even crazier. You should never have got involved with him in the first place. I made that mistake. But I got out quick – soon as I found out what he was really like. You'd better do the same. You're no match for him, Princess. He's nastier and more scheming than your little brain can ever imagine.

Katy B, why did you get that horrible rough girl Emily to write me a note? You told her what to say, didn't you? Cos she said the same as you, that Cooper wouldn't change. Just stop ganging up on me! Leave me alone! You don't give people a chance do you? You only see the bad things in everyone. Well, Coop knows he was wrong. He sent me a present with that card, a lovely gold crucifix. He said it cost him £45. But I didn't show it to you because I know you'd just say he's playing games or he stole it or something. I'm wearing it now. If you look up you can see it, outside my shirt. And don't send me any more notes. I told you, I'm not listening to you any more. If you send them I'll tear them up and if you try to talk to me at break I'll just put my hands over my ears and run away from you. Besides, Coop does not like me talking to you. He says you are a bad influence.

Dexie, this is Chrissie Parker again. Why did you bang your head on your desk like that when you read the note that I just sent you asking if you would meet Sophie tonight outside McDonald's? You will give yourself a terrible headache, you will damage your brains! Anyway, Sophie wants to know, does banging your head all those times on the desk mean yes or no. Tick below.

YES	
NO	

TO DEXIE URGENT. FROM KATY B.

This is serious, Dexie. Try to talk some sense into J. He has gone crazy. He says Cooper killed his Belgian hares last night and that he is going to get him for it. You know as well as I do that he doesn't stand a chance against Cooper. You've got to stop him. He'll get hurt. He'll end up in Casualty. Please try to stop him, he is just sending my notes back unopened.

RETURN TO KATY B.

I'm not even opening your note. You can stick your note. I don't need to open it cos I already know what it says. It says, "Dexie, will you go out with Sophie?" That's right, isn't it? That's what it says. Have you all gone deaf or something? Why won't anyone listen when I say NO? How else can I say it? Non, nein, niet, NO!

Chapter Fourteen
English

PASS TO KATY B. URGENT

Katy, this is J. You heard the news? It's all over the school. Tried to see you at lunch, couldn't find you. It's amazing! Cooper and Ant were fighting, yeah, and Cooper's been beaten and everyone saw it! Yeah I know, I wouldn't have believed it either. I didn't think Ant would've stood a chance against Cooper except I was there, Katy, I saw it with my own eyes. And I loved every single minute of it, it was class. And I was cheering louder than anyone else when Cooper went down. Well, he had it coming. He deserved everything he got.

Don't know what they were fighting about – thought they were best mates. But it doesn't matter what started it. All that matters is that Cooper lost and now he's Mr Nobody and he can't hold his head up in the school and even the tiny kids don't respect him. His reputation's shot! Look at him over there in the corner, he's a wreck. Bet he was as surprised as everyone else that he lost. Look, there's cuts on his face from Ant's fists and blood on his shirt collar. He's tried to wash it out but you can still see it. Look at those bruises!

This is what happened. It was out on the football field. We're all round them in a ring really excited and yelling and shouting and at first it looks like Cooper's winning so they all cheer for him, "COOP-ER! COOP-ER!" Ant's staggering about and they all think he's finished. But then he kicks out WHAM! a real sledgehammer, catches Coop smack on the side of the head and Coop goes sprawling and then Ant follows it up with a kick to his jaw and Cooper goes down, KER-RASH! like a mighty tree falling and can't get up again.

When they see Cooper's finished, course everybody changes sides and cheers like mad for Ant, "ANT! ANT!", they're going wild! And they're all yelling, "Kill 'im Ant!" and Ant dusts off his hands real cool and moves in for the kill but then the teachers come running and everybody scatters. Except some of us carry Ant off on our shoulders like he's King, just leave Cooper face down in the mud and now Ant rules the school. It's fantastic, better than anything I could have done to him – Cooper's TOTALLY humiliated. And I love it. I love it!

Look at him Katy, he's finished. Go on, go on, STARE at him if you like, don't be scared. He won't do nothing. It's not like before when he'd say, "Who you looking at!" if you even took a peek at him. Now HE daren't look US in the eye! And look at that massive cut on his chin! Surprised his jaw isn't smashed like glass. Bet it hurts like hell. Good. Time he suffered some pain for a change. Pity his neck wasn't snapped same as he did to my Belgian hare. She was beautiful she was, remember her velvet coat, remember how she ran? Best I ever had, I'll never get the chance of another like her.

Supposed to be doing an essay about Advantages and Disadvantages of School Uniform – yawn. Only written the date so far.

Don't send me a note back. Pottsie's stopped marking now, she'll catch you for sure.

Chapter Fifteen

Detention

About time, Spenser's gone back in the stock cupboard. Don't talk – just write notes. He can still hear us.

Honest, it's not fair, is it Katy B? Why did he put us 2 in detention and no one else? Everybody passes notes in Maths, it's been going on like FOREVER and then today he freaks out about it and puts us in detention. And it's not as if it stops us doing Maths is it? I can write notes and do Maths at the same time. Easy peasy. I tried to tell him that. But he just yelled even more. He'll give himself a heart attack if he doesn't lighten up. Can't understand teachers, can you Katy B? They're not like NORMAL people, they're totally unreasonable. And why did he pick on us 2, it's not fair is it? Sophie was writing notes, I saw her, but Sophie is teacher's pet. She makes me squirm, she says, "Sir, Maths is my most favourite subject." Yuk! He'd never put her in detention. And he's scared of Emily. He wouldn't pick on her, she's got bigger muscles than him. How many lines have we got to write? Did he say 50 or 100? He won't ask to see them, he never does.

Did U hear, me and Dexie are back together again. I'm wearing his ring – look how sparkly it is.

I can't keep up with your love life, Rach. Thought you'd given up boys for good.

Yes, but this is Dexie, isn't it? Everyone expects us to be together. It's like RachelandDexie. When we broke up people kept saying, "It's really weird seeing you on your own without Dexie. It doesn't look right," because we'd been together like FOREVER. And Dexie said something funny. When I said, sort of casual, as if I didn't care, "Dexie, what about us 2 getting back together again," he said, "At least I'll be safe then." What's he mean? Safe from who? Is anyone giving him aggravation cos if they are I'd like to know cos they've got to answer to ME!
I must not pass notes in class
I must not pass notes in class.
Phew that was close. Did you see? Spense stuck his head out the stock cupboard. Thought he was going to come over! It's OK, he's gone back inside.

So now you're back with Dexie everything's just like before?

Yep, we're still arguing.

I don't mean that. I'm talking about what happened. About when you thought you were pregnant. Don't you remember? What a bad time it was and how you didn't know what to do and—

I'm not going to read any more of your note! You're preaching again Katy B. It's a real bad habit you've got. I told you I want to forget all about that. Why do you want to remind me of bad times when everything is working out OK and it is a good time now? And the summer holidays are next week and I'm really happy because life is great for a change. Anyhow, it won't happen again, we'll be careful or something. It's just like you, Katy. Why can't you forget about all the other bad stuff and just say – IT'S BRILLIANT THAT U AND DEXIE R TOGETHER AGAIN!! Instead of being a boring old spoilsport.

OK I give up. IT'S BRILLIANT THAT U AND DEXIE R TOGETHER AGAIN!! There, is that OK?

That's better, Katy. That's a nice note instead of a depressing one. Now let's just write about NICE things shall we?

I must not pass notes in class
I wish he'd stay in the stock cupboard instead of popping in and out like a Jack in the Box. He's interrupting my note writing. So, where are you going for your holidays Katy? We're going self-catering in Turkey.

J and his Mum have got a caravan at the seaside in Cornwall. They asked me to go with them.

What, not abroad?

No, you idiot, in Cornwall.

What, not even abroad! You're not going are you? You won't get a very good tan, not like I will in Turkey. It's scorching hot there in summer.

What happened about France? Thought you were camping in France with Lisa and her mum and dad?
I must not pass notes in class.

Not now, that sort of fizzled out. I don't see Lisa much any more.

Is she still with Cooper? Bet she's not. He's nothing now, not after he got beat in that fight and everybody saw it. Where is he anyhow? Not surprised he daren't show his face in school. Even the little kids aren't scared of him! I saw this skinny little kid the other day laugh in his face "Ha, ha, ha!" just like that. And Coop didn't do nothing about it. Just turned his back and walked away.

Don't ask me what Lisa's doing. I don't know these days. She doesn't tell me.

So what about you and J. Are U 2 still together? Is it serious?

I don't know about that either. We're still together and we get on really well. But he doesn't say much. Not about what he feels about us or anything.

Why don't U ask him then?

Oh right! Good idea! What am I supposed to do? Just come straight out with it and say, "J, are we serious? Do you like me a lot or do you just like me a little bit or

aren't you interested? Or what?" How could I do that? It'd be really embarrassing!

Write it in a note! U can say things in notes U can't say face to face. Here, I'll do you an example. I will make it ever so tactful. See below.

Look J, I am fed up not knowing where I stand. So answer the question below or else.

QUESTION: What do you feel about Katy B?

KEY

I fancy her like mad 
I fancy her
I like her a lot
I like her
I like her a bit
I haven't made up my mind yet
I'm not interested

Answer ______________________________

Honestly Rach I can't send him that!

Why not, it's a good note. I've made it really simple for him. He doesn't even have to write anything. All he's got to do is draw a little picture. And you get to know where you stand. Easy peasy. Everybody's happy!

But it's like he's got to sit an exam or something. And how can he say what he feels just by drawing a picture?

What do you have to make things complicated for Katy? That is asking for trouble. You think too much, that's your problem. OK then, if you insist, just leave a bit of space at the end and put ANY OTHER COMMENTS then he can write some other stuff if he wants to. But I bet he doesn't! Satisfied now? Oh God, here comes Spenser, start writing lines quick!
I must
I must not
I must not pass
I must not pass notes in

Chapter Sixteen
Science

PASS TO KATY B.

Katy, this is Lisa, surprise, surprise. Know I haven't been in touch for ages. But it's the holidays tomorrow and I won't see you for ever such a long time so I've got to send you one last note to tell you that Coop is still ringing me up – whoops, Mr Walker's giving me the evil eye. What's wrong with teachers? Have you noticed Katy that the closer it gets to the holidays the meaner they get? They should be going wild, like we are! It's sooo mean making us sit quiet on the LAST DAY. We weren't going VERY wild were we? Hasn't he got a sense of humour? There's hardly any silly string left in his hair.

How dare he the creep? How dare Cooper keep threatening you? Hope you slammed the phone down on him, hope you told him to get lost. He's Mr Nobody now, you don't need to be scared of him any more. Rachel saw this little kid (this really little kid) laughing

at him, going Ha Ha Ha! And Cooper just turned around and walked away!

No, Katy B, you don't understand. It's not like you think. He wasn't threatening me or anything. He was phoning me up to ask for some advice.

What are you talking about Lisa? What kind of game is he playing now? Asking for ADVICE! After the way he treated you. After what he did to J's Belgian hares. He's a total scum bag. You didn't TALK to him did you Lisa? Write me another note quick, tell me you didn't.

That's what I wanted to tell you, Katy B, it wasn't Coop that killed J's rabbits. Ant did it, to teach J a lesson. Coop got really mad and told Ant he shouldn't have done it. Ant said, "I thought you'd be pleased" and he went berserk and he attacked Coop. And Coop didn't expect it – Ant was supposed to be his best mate! He just couldn't believe Ant would make a move against him. He was really shocked. So he lost the fight.

Lisa, haven't you learned anything? Cooper was lying about the rabbits. I bet it was him. J says it was.

Cooper's got no friends, he's nothing now, so he's just trying to get some sympathy. Bet he even wants you to go out with him again! Tell him to get lost!

It's not like you think Katy B. Honest it's not. Watch out, Walker's nosing around.

I don't care if he's nosing around – I can't believe you Lisa, are you CRAZY? I know, you're still scared of Cooper, aren't you? That's what it is. He IS threatening you isn't he, the creep?

NO HE **ISN'T**. You aren't listening to me, Katy B. You never listen. I just told you he's not, didn't I? Don't you even READ my notes? Look, I know what I'm doing right? Me and Cooper are NOT going out. Right? I told him I'd never go out with him, no chance, it is finished between us. And he said, "That's OK. I didn't expect you to." And anyway, I'm going out with Daniel Stephenson from 10Y again (Surprise! You didn't know about that, did you Katy? He called me up and said, "I still like you." And I said, "I still like you. I must have been crazy to finish you." So we're going out again, isn't that brilliant?) But anyway, the point is, Coop knows about Daniel. I've told him. But he STILL calls me up. And we just talk. He doesn't threaten me or pester me or nothing. And I'm not scared of him any more.

So what's he want then?

Just to chat. I told you.

Chat? Cooper never CHATTED to people before, he just thumped them! Don't trust him, Lisa. Keep away from him. Anyhow what's he want to CHAT about, the weather, or something? For Heaven's sake!

I **TOLD** you, he wants some advice, he wants me to help him. What's so amazing about that? There's this girl he's going out with. See, told you he didn't want me as a girlfriend. She's called Caroline – I don't know her, she goes to another school. And he's asking me how to treat her. What to say to her, where to take her out, that kind of stuff. It's like he's scared of making the same mistakes he did with me. Like he wants everything to work out this time. We talk and talk for ages, Katy B. Not just about his girlfriend but about all kinds of things. That's all it is – just talking.

It's weird, what do you want to talk to HIM for? You could talk to ME. I mean, this is sick talking to COOPER. Giving him advice and all that. Even sounds like you're getting quite FRIENDLY! It's too weird to even think about. How can you be FRIENDS with someone like him?

He's not that bad, Katy B. He's all right really, you don't know him. He's trying to be different, he's trying to change, he really is.

This is crazy! He's horrible, he's a big bully, the whole world knows that. He's a snake – people like him don't change. I feel sorry for that poor girl Caroline. Still, at least it gets you off the hook if he's got some other girl to threaten.

BUT IT'S NOT LIKE THAT! Look, this is useless, Katy B. Don't let's fight, it's the last day. We'll never agree about

Cooper. Just trust me to get things right. You never trusted me to get things right on my own did you? I can, ya know! I'm grown up now, ya know! Coop thinks I am cos we talk about all kinds of things, really serious important things sometimes.

You're right Lisa. We shouldn't fight. We're friends aren't we. Still friends?

Course we are, Katy B. We've been friends since we were little. I couldn't not be friends with you.

Chapter Seventeen
Science

PASS TO J PRESCOTT

Holidays tomorrow. Can't wait, can you J? Bye Lisa and Cooper! Bye Rachel and Dexie and Sophie and everyone else. I need to Relaaaaax and build sand castles. Just get away from all their schemes and secrets and notes that say, "Katy B, you're smart, what's the answer to this?" From breaking up and making up and problems and dramas and disasters. Feels like we've been on a roller coaster ride this term. One that leaves you shaky and dizzy with your head whirling round. I want life to be nice and PEACEFUL and CALM for a change. Don't want to see a single one of them. Least, not until we get back from Cornwall.

Well you won't see them will you? Cos we're all splitting up for the holidays, going all over the world. Sophie's going to Florida – some people get all the luck. And Lisa's going to

France and Rachel's going to Turkey. And we're off to Cornwall in a caravan.

Just our luck, Emily or someone'll turn up in the caravan next to ours.

Emily won't. She's not going anywhere this summer. Her mum's out of work and they can't afford it. Hey, forgot to tell you, I got the chance of another Belgian Hare. This breeder I know is going to sell me one.

Anyway, thought you got on OK with Emily?

That's because she's not as Big and Bad as she tries to make out. She doesn't say much or write notes much. But she's smart, a lot smarter than me. And when she writes notes, you better read em. She's all right – long as you keep out her way when she starts throwing punches.
PS. Brilliant about the Belgian Hare!

What about Lisa. You'll miss her, won't you? Thought you two were, like, INSEPARABLE.

I'll miss her, I suppose. We're still friends. But we're not that close any more. Maybe we never were as close as I thought.

What's happening with her and Cooper? Heard he still phones her up. Heard he tells her his problems, like she's the Samaritans or something. What's going on there? It's weird. He hurts people. He messes up their lives. She's crazy even talking to him. You're her friend, Katy B, you should tell her!

I've tried. I think it's weird too. I've talked to her, written loads of notes. Doesn't make no difference. She says she knows Cooper better than we do. Says she knows what she's doing and to leave her alone.

He's a bastard. He killed my Belgian hares.

Lisa says he didn't. She says it was Ant. J, do you think it's true that Cooper's changed?

Is that supposed to be a joke, Katy B?

I don't know. I can't worry about Lisa any more. Emily's right – what she wrote in that note. I tore it up but I still remember it. She said to back off, let Lisa sort things out herself.

But you were only trying to be a good friend! Stop her messing up her life!

Maybe, I don't know. Maybe she needs to do things for herself. Emily says if she wants my help she'll ask for it.

Yeah, ask you to pick up the pieces you mean!

Maybe she knows what she's doing, like she says. Maybe she's right about Cooper. Ever thought about that?

You're full of jokes this morning, aren't you, Katy B?

Anyhow I'm not going to worry about it NO MORE. Not until AFTER the holiday. I really need a break. And

nobody's got to write me a single note. If someone's in trouble, or got any hot news, I don't want a note about it. At least, not until school starts again on 5th September.

Just one last note Katy B. Cos you can write things in notes you can't say face-to-face. Things you can't say out loud. So here goes.

I LOVE YOU KATY B.

Quick, rip this note up and throw it away now you've read it. My mates will give me a really hard time if they see what it says.

I promise no one will ever read it. Not your mates, not anyone but me. Look, I'll fold it up really small, put it in my shirt pocket. I just can't throw it away like you said. Not the only note worth keeping.

Love Katy B.

Hi Katy B! Guess who? Yes, you're right! ☺ I saw you and J writing lots of notes to each other and once he looked really serious. Are you sick of him Katy B? Have you just dumped him? Cos if you have will you pass him on to me? I will do you a BIG FAVOUR and take him off your hands. Cos I am that kind of girl. I just love doing BIG FAVOURS for my bestest friends. So send him a note for me quick before someone else grabs him. You send it as I do not want to seem too keen do I! Here, I will write the note for you.

CUT HERE ✂- -

SMILE JONATHAN! DO NOT BE HEART-BROKEN! IT IS YOUR LUCKY DAY! SOPHIE ☺ IS BETWEEN BOYFRIENDS AT THE MOMENT AND SHE WILL MEET YOU TONITE 7 O'CLOCK OUTSIDE MCDONALDS

CUT HERE ✂- -

DO NOT SEND ME ANY MORE NOTES SOPHIE. RIGHT? IS THAT ABSOLUTELY CLEAR? I HAVE GIVEN UP NOTES FOR THE SUMMER.

Signed Katy B.

PS. J is not available, we are still together. So hands off.

No need to be so rude, Katy B. It was just a genuine mistake, that's all. I was just trying to do you a favour, that's all. But even if you are rude, you cannot upset me. I am still your bestest friend.

I will send you a note when school starts again. When you open that very first note on September 5th, it will be from guess who? Yes from ME!

CRISS
CROSS

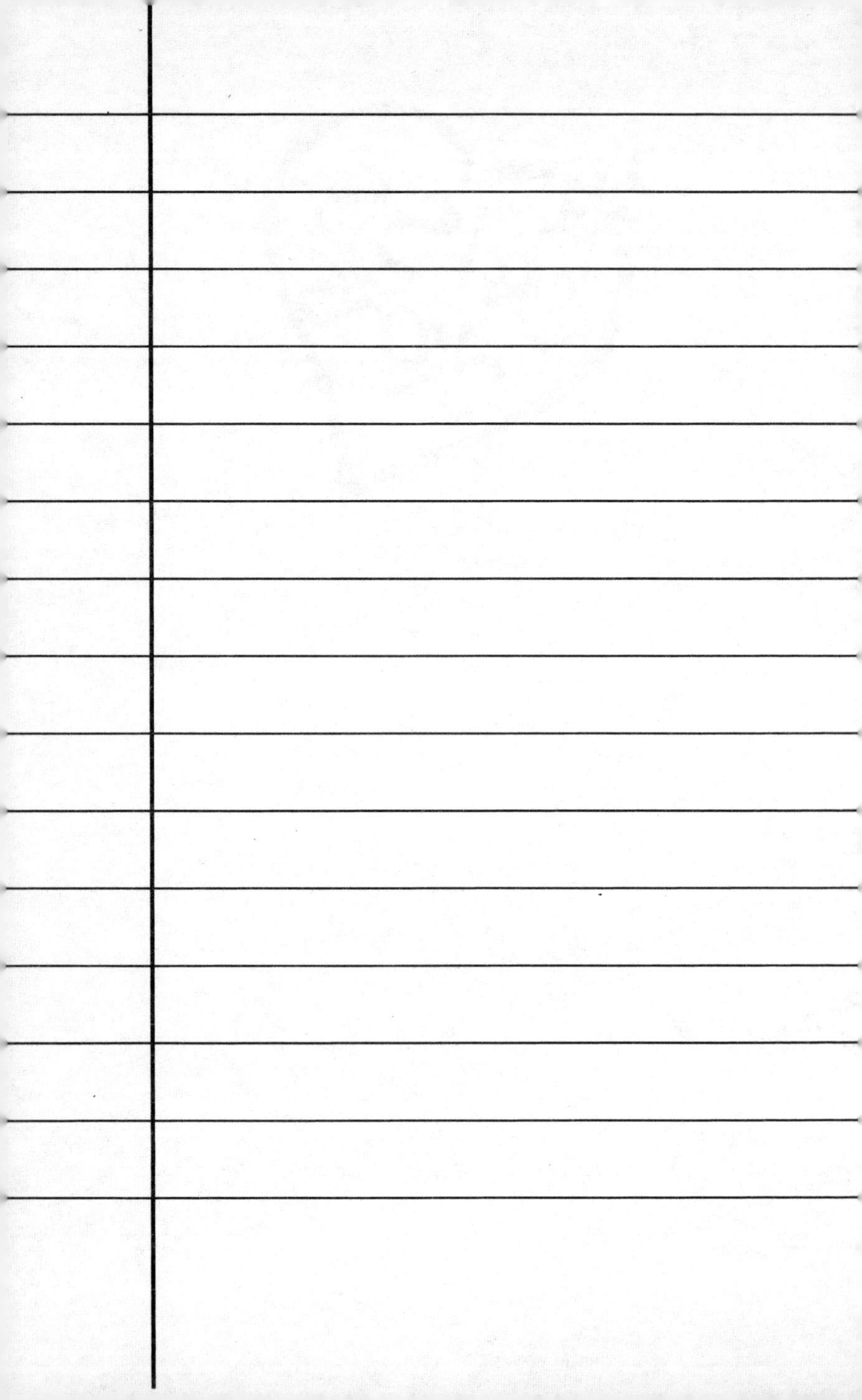

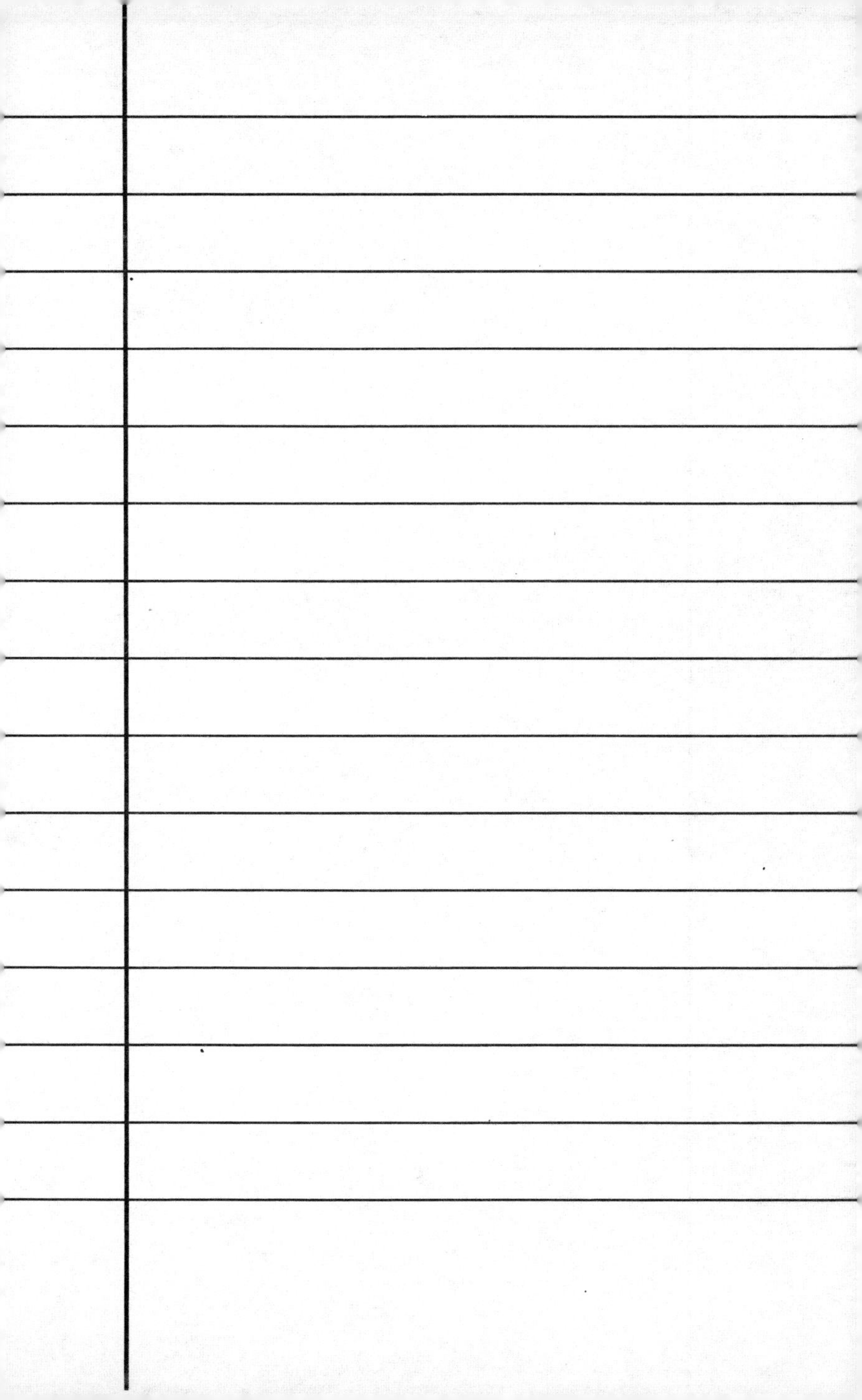

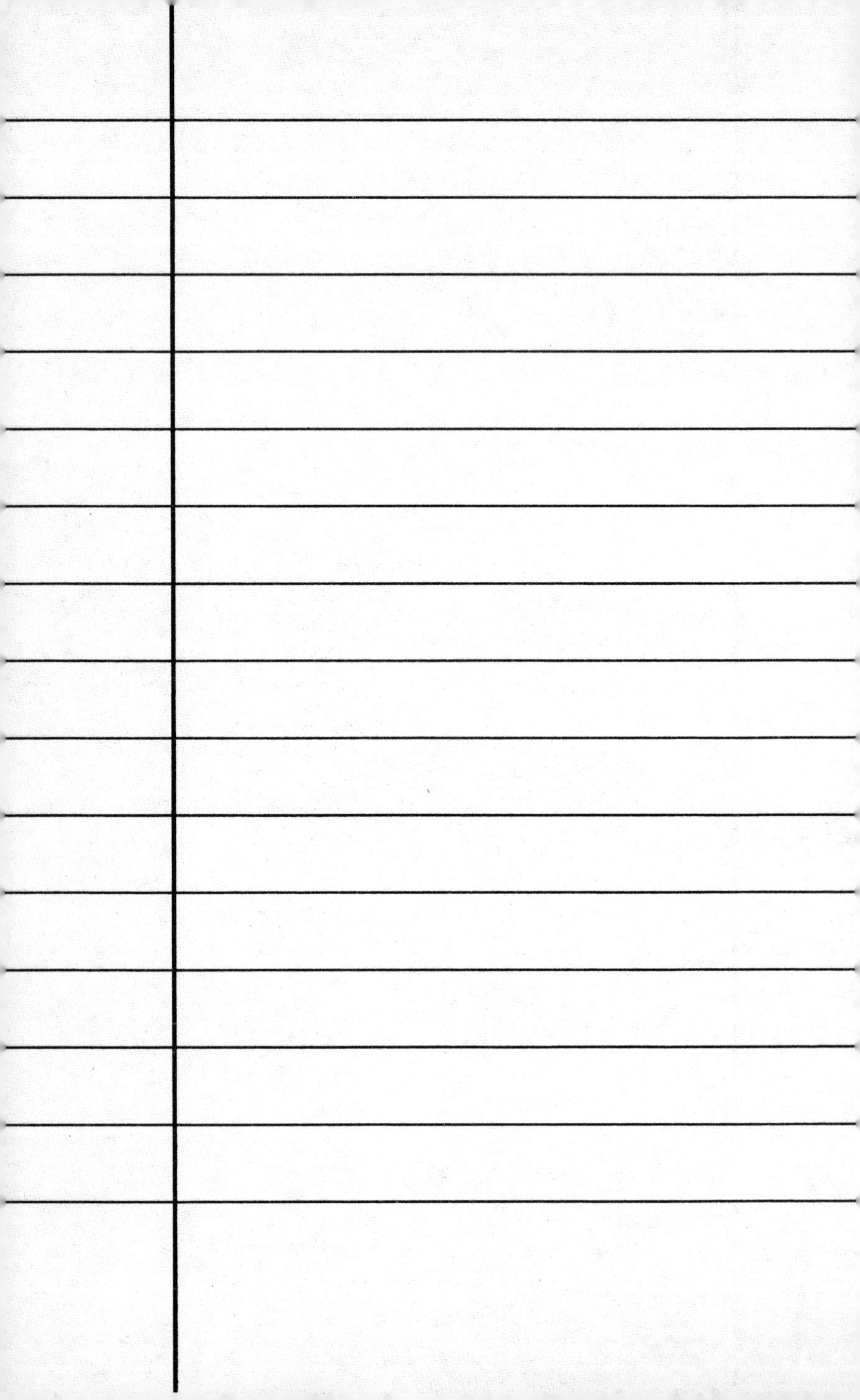

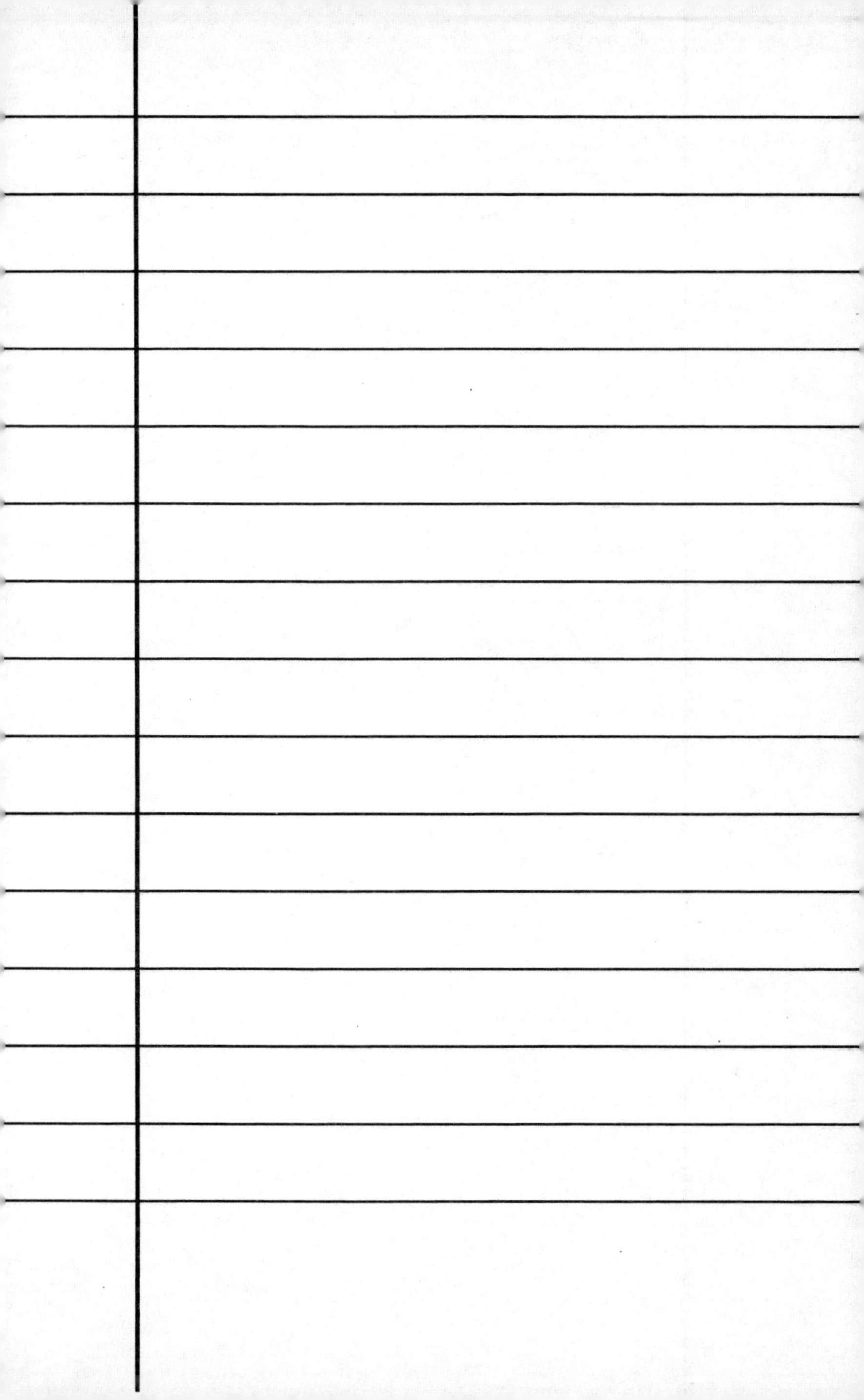

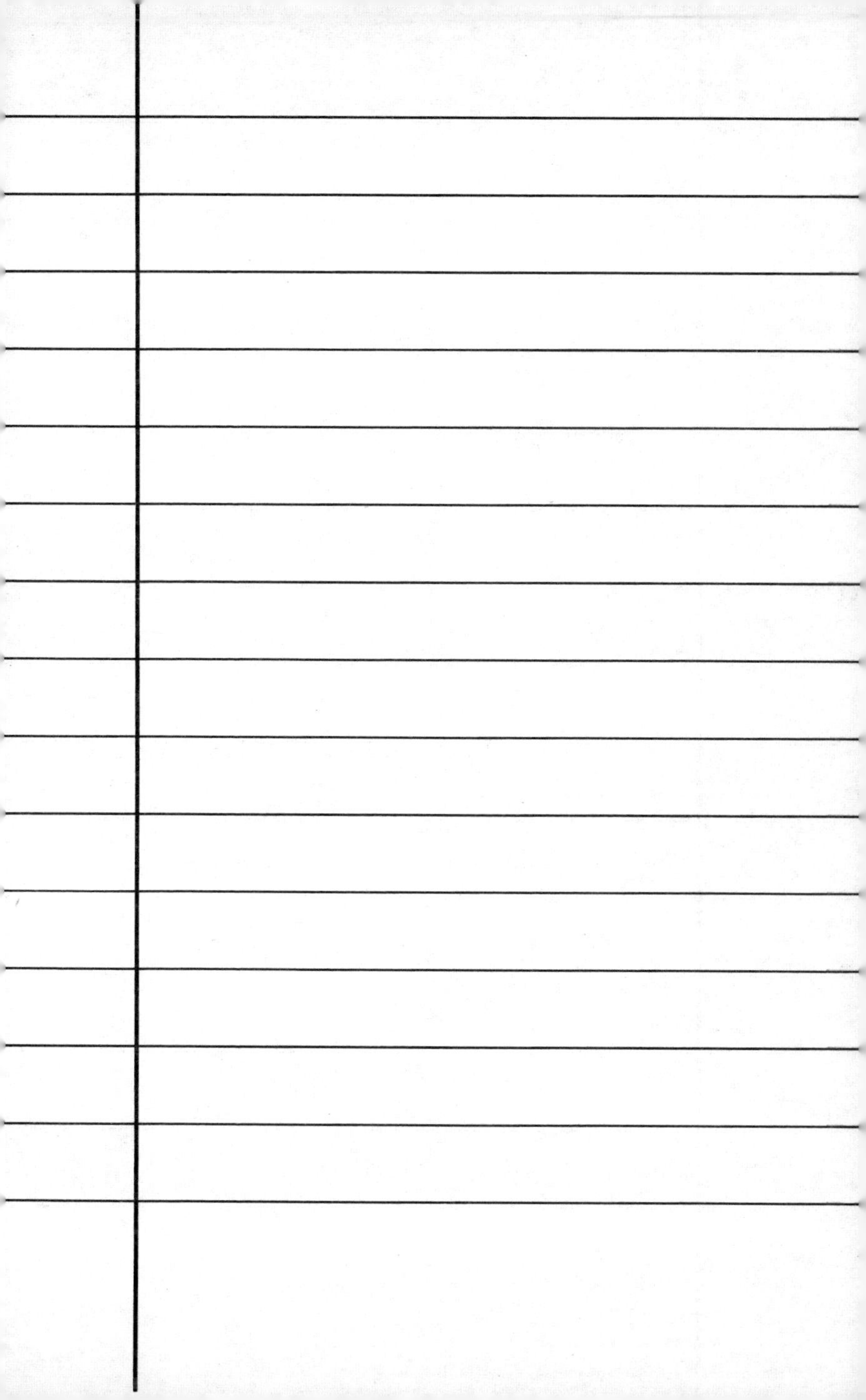

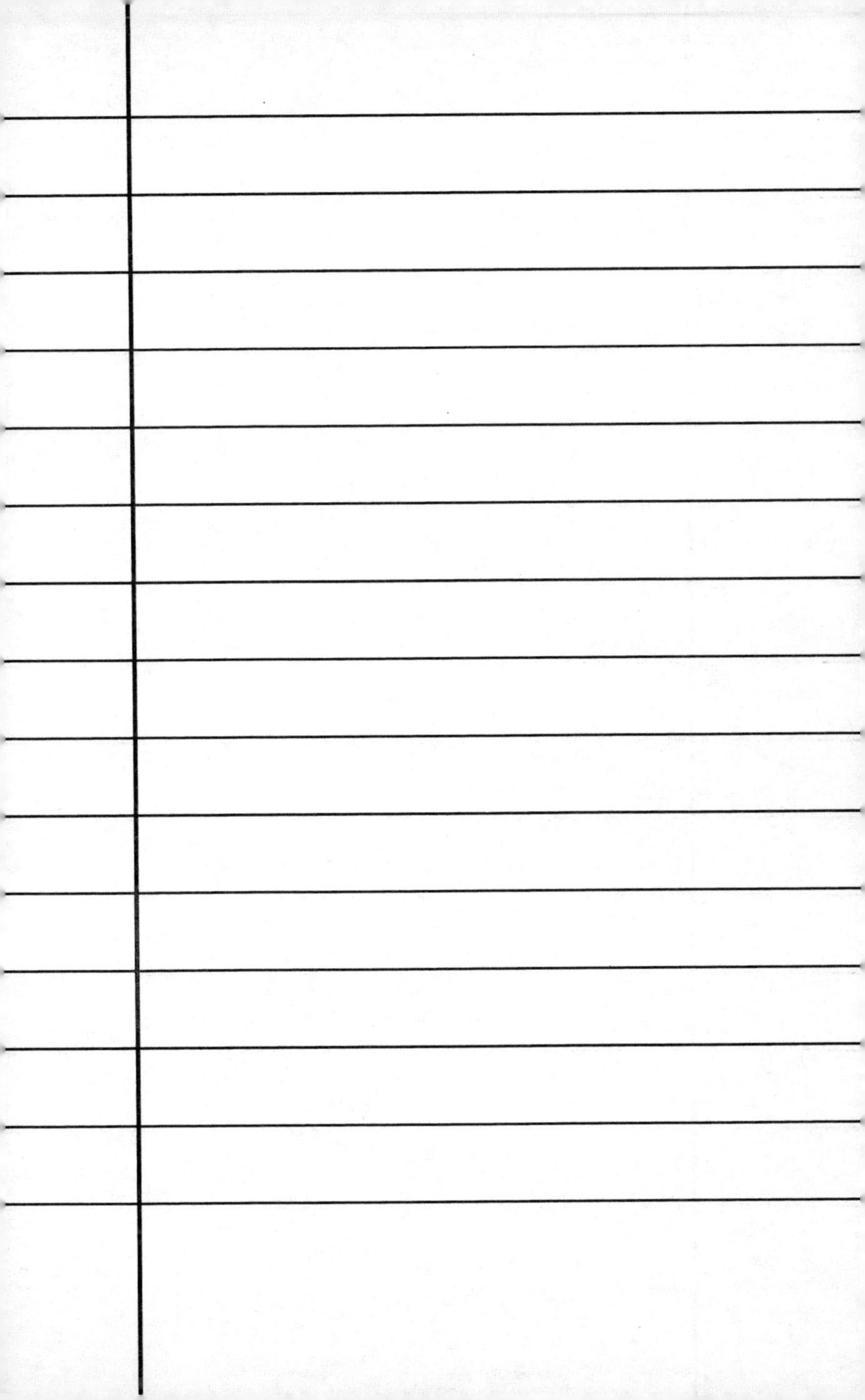

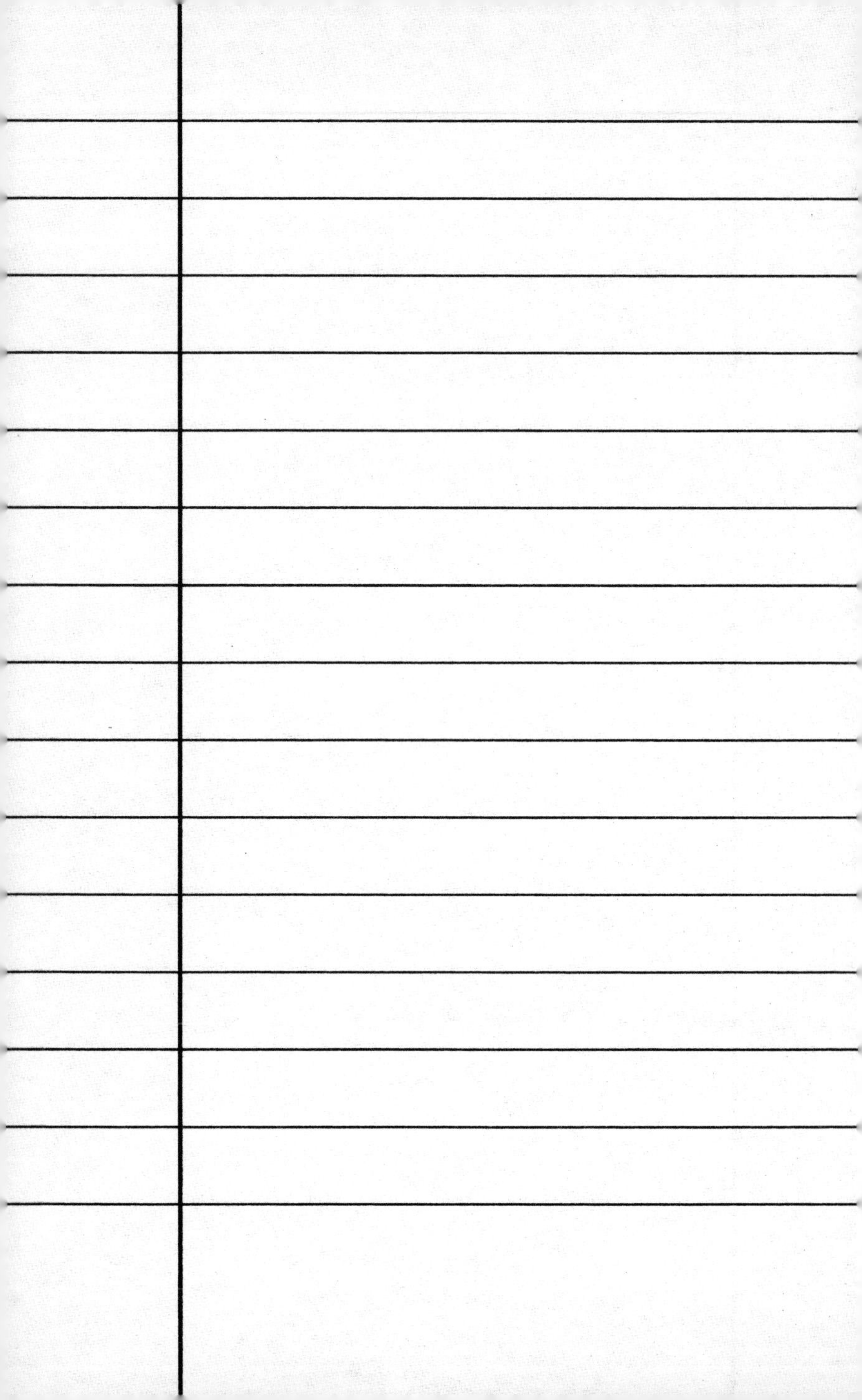

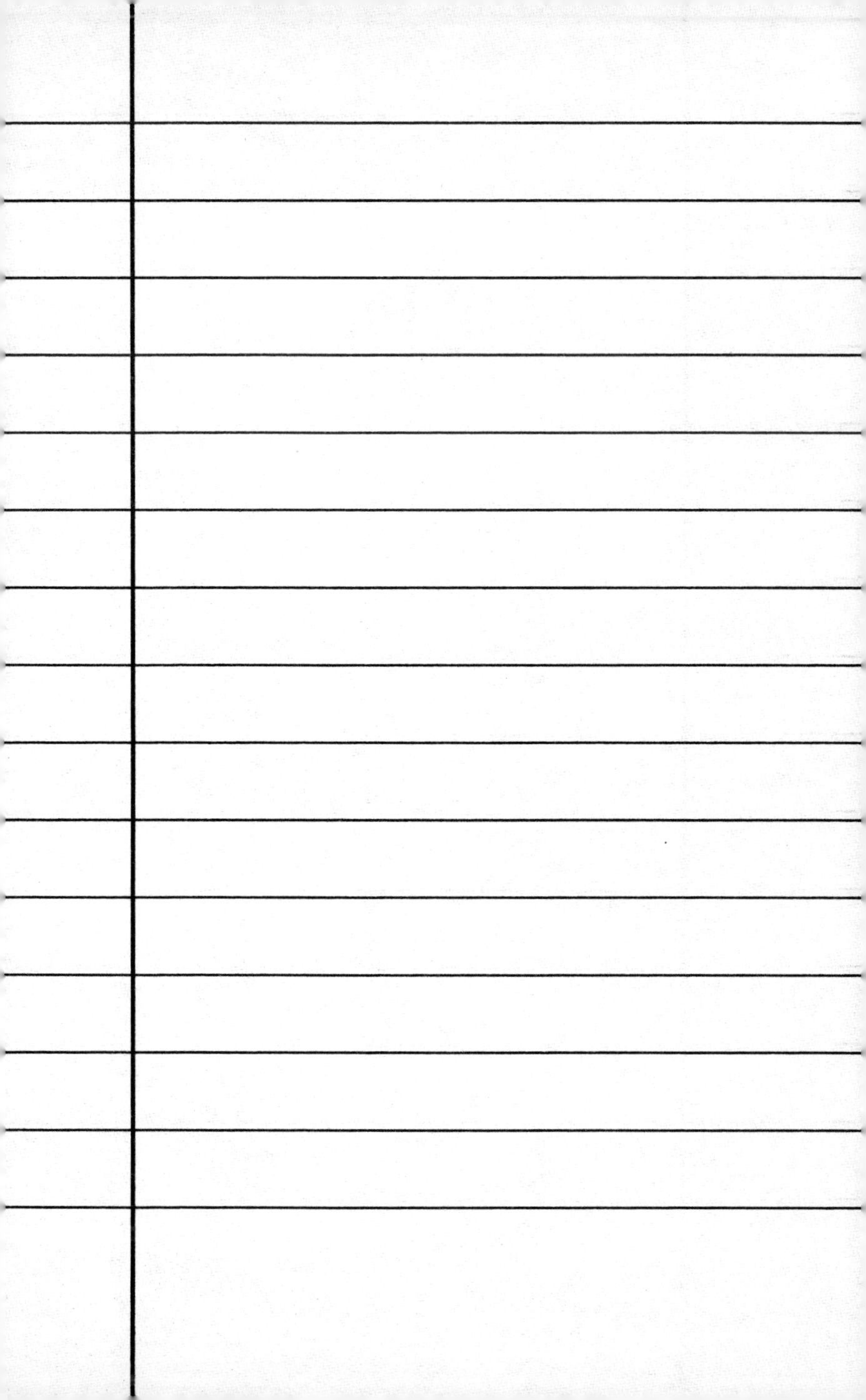

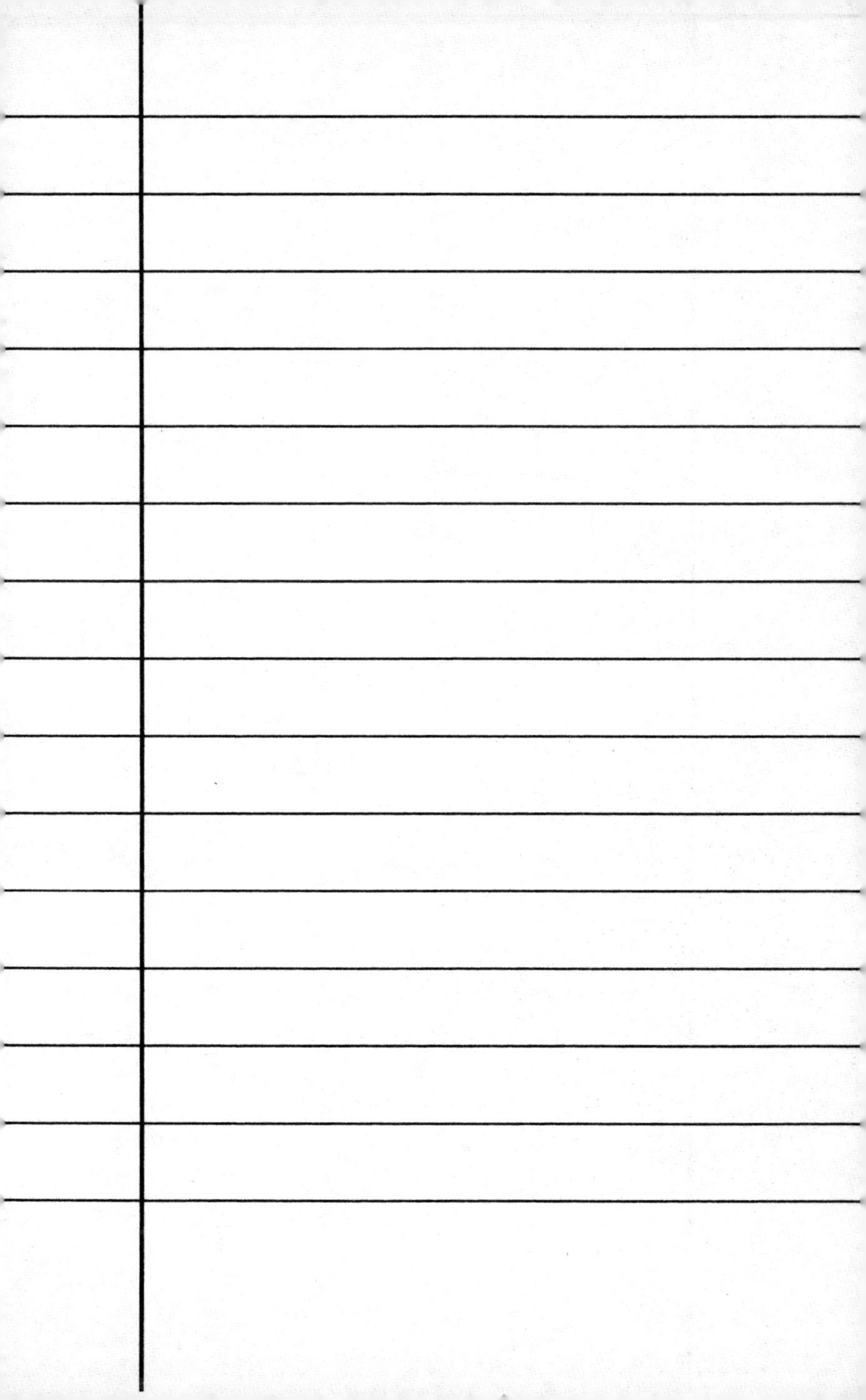

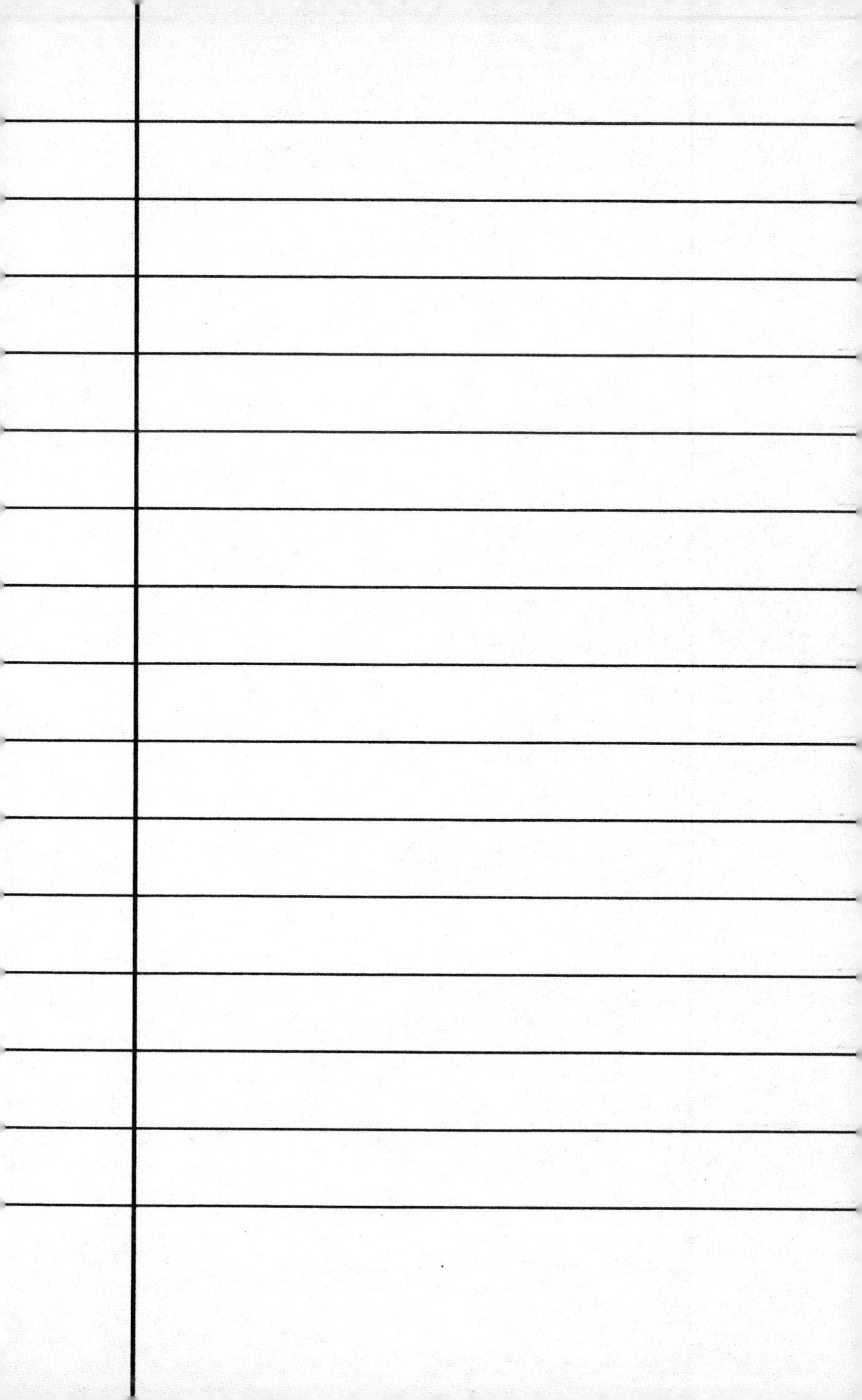